*A Candlelight
Ecstasy Romance* ®

**"YOU'RE NOT LEAVING! YOU'RE MY
WIFE AND I WANT TO KNOW THAT
WHEN I COME HOME, YOU'LL BE HERE!"
GARRET STORMED.**

"It isn't enough." Her voice caught.

"I know. I'm never around. I admit it! But isn't our time
together enough?"

She didn't reply. She'd already said it all.

"You're killing me. Do you realize that?"

"Don't."

"You say 'don't' to me? How can *you* do this to us? Am
I so meaningless to you? Or do you want another man?"

"You know there's no one else, Garret," she answered
quietly.

He turned from her, his head down as he stared at the
floor. "I don't understand you. You're just throwing it all
away. And me with it," he accused bitterly.

"Oh, Garret, I'm not leaving *you,* just the situation
. . ." Her eyes filled, begging him to understand.

"All right. If that's the way you want it, it's done. I
don't want an unwilling wife. Discontented and unfulfilled. Leave. Good-bye!"

A CANDLELIGHT ECSTASY ROMANCE ®

THE DEDICATED MAN

Lass Small

A CANDLELIGHT ECSTASY ROMANCE ®

Published by
Dell Publishing Co., Inc.
1 Dag Hammarskjold Plaza
New York, New York 10017

Dell ® TM 681510, Dell Publishing Co., Inc.

Candlelight Ecstasy Romance®, 1,203,540, is a registered
trademark of Dell Publishing Co., Inc.,
New York, New York.

ISBN: 0–440–11837–9

Printed in the United States of America
First printing—November 1983

To Bill

To Our Readers:

We have been delighted with your enthusiastic response to Candlelight Ecstasy Romances®, and we thank you for the interest you have shown in this exciting series.

In the upcoming months we will continue to present the distinctive sensuous love stories you have come to expect only from Ecstasy. We look forward to bringing you many more books from your favorite authors and also the very finest work from new authors of contemporary romantic fiction.

As always, we are striving to present the unique, absorbing love stories that you enjoy most—books that are more than ordinary romance.

Your suggestions and comments are always welcome. Please write to us at the address below.

Sincerely,

The Editors
Candlelight Romances
1 Dag Hammarskjold Plaza
New York, New York 10017

CHAPTER ONE

The first time that Piper Morling saw Garret Raymond was at an informal dance on one of the piers on Lake Springfield, just after her graduation from high school.

He was in a group of people, and she simply stared at the tall, blond, tan, older man. In all of her eighteen years she had never seen a man who'd made her stare. It was obvious to her that he was a stranger, because in Bible-belt, small-city, conservative Springfield it seemed as if everyone knew everyone else through politics, the DAR, the normal schools, the University and, of course, kinship.

So when Piper saw Garret, she had asked Celia Parker, "Who is he?" Ceel would know because her mother was such a nosy woman that Piper's father called her Parker the Barker. Ceel said, "Garret Raymond. But forget it. He belongs to Barb Tallman."

But Piper couldn't tear her eyes from him, and eventually when his glance met hers, he studied her as openly— and he winked. She'd blushed, but as she'd turned away she had smiled rather breathlessly.

She was so aware of him, she knew his exact location in the room by instinct alone. She didn't look at him too often, but when she did, he was watching her, and he was amused. She became very self-conscious, acting more animatedly than usual and laughing a lot.

But later, when she looked for him, he wasn't there. Oh, no. Had he left? He couldn't have, and she started to turn to search further when a deeply thrilling masculine voice said in her ear, "Looking for someone?" And it was Garret.

She did all the idiotic things. She blushed and stammered, and her tongue took over. "Oh, hi. You're Garret Raymond, aren't you." He nodded, amused. "I'm Piper Morling," she rattled on. "Are you visiting?" And through extreme will power, she managed to shut up, but she looked up at him with her heart in her blue, thickly lashed eyes.

Her dark hair was pulled back and tied with a ribbon that matched the pale blue in her printed India cotton dress that hugged her shapely body. Her lips were softly parted, because her nose didn't seem to be working right and she wasn't getting enough air. Her heart was hammering along so fast that she knew the reverberations were jiggling the ties of her dress across her chest.

He asked her to dance, and she reached for him, but what happened after that wasn't too clear to her. They danced and her feet were remarkably obedient, and a part of her mind marveled over that. The entire surface of her skin was extremely conscious of him and her muscles were painfully tensed. She tried to sigh casually, to relax and unwind the tense muscles in her shoulders, but that only pushed her breasts closer against him.

She was acutely aware of his body and that his arm was a strong band holding her. She'd never been so glad she was a woman—however new she was at it. But she thought she had all the symptoms of a heart attack, and she wondered if he'd be embarrassed when she passed out and the ambulance had to come for her.

He talked to her, and she must have sounded coherent, but some separate part of her mind was managing that by itself, and she wasn't in touch with which part, or even what was being said.

A slow lover's dance was next and, since she didn't even offer to let him go, they danced that one too. The lights were low, and she sighed and simply relaxed against him, her body soft and yielding, her head on his shoulder. He held her there, with his cheek pressed against the side of her head. It was just lovely.

When the music ended much too soon, she turned her face up to his, and they just looked at each other. Then when the other couples drifted from the dance floor, he led her to the drink stand instead of returning her to her friends, and it thrilled her that he'd wanted to stay with her.

She was under legal age for beer, so he bought her a 7-Up which she tilted carelessly and dribbled right down her chest. She was appalled. He grinned and helped her dry the spill. She knew she must be coming down with something dreadful to feel so feverish and, as he touched her, there was a very strange feeling in the pit of her stomach that licked around like a fireball.

She was so sticky from the spilled drink that she went to the rest room to wash her hands and chest. Garret had suggested that, and she'd smiled effusively at him, as though he'd been brilliant to think of it. Barb Tallman was in the rest room and she was furious about something that Piper didn't readily understand and she wasn't terribly interested in having it explained to her. But Barb made herself quite clear. "You stay away from Garret Raymond! He's mine!"

Other than being rather amazed that someone else seemed to claim him, Piper appeared unmoved by the outburst and Barb stormed out. The rest of the evening was passed in a gauzelike, magic haze.

The day after the dance, Piper was a little closer to reality, but her ravings about Garret Raymond caused her two younger sisters, Arlene and Jennifer, to heave theatrical sighs in disgust. Her two brothers were spared her ramblings as they had gone off to fish. Piper gushed about how gorgeous Garret was, that he was the perfect dancer. His gray eyes . . . and she flung herself around as if mortally wounded, and her sisters laughed. Mrs. Morling sewed peacefully. Being a true romantic, she knew that as long as Piper was that noisy about Garret, it didn't mean much.

The family had a pier anchored in a secluded cove along the river at the bottom of their land, and just before lunch Piper went down there to sunbathe, telling the almost sixteen-year-old Arlene to be sure to bring the suntan lotion, since she couldn't carry that too.

Piper climbed down the riverbank and stepped onto the floating pier that was supported by empty oil drums, causing it to tilt. She set down the radio, the timer, a thermos of lemonade, and her towels, untied her top, and lay on her stomach with a straw hat plopped over her head.

It was very quiet. She heard Arlene coming and Piper yelled, "Did you bring the suntan lotion?"

"Yes . . . uh . . ." Whatever else Arlene was going to say, she'd apparently changed her mind, but when she stepped onto the floating pier, that end sank, and the other end of the pier tilted precariously.

Piper clutched at the side and scolded, "Be careful! These things can turn over, you know!"

Her sister made only some sounds.

As if continuing an interrupted conversation, Piper then went on. "That man! Garret Raymond. Isn't that a beautiful name? My God." And she groaned. "I'd like to drag him into the bushes and . . . ravish him!"

Again there were only sounds from her sister.

Piper put her own interpretation on them and agreed. "Yeah, I know, if I did force myself on him, Dad'd kill him. But it might be worth it. He'd die happy, and it would save him from Barb Tallman."

The float tilted crazily, and Piper exclaimed crossly, "For Pete's sake, Arlene, what are you trying to do?" She got up on her hands and knees, leaving her top on the boards below her, and pushed back the straw hat to look inquiringly around for her sister—and saw Arlene struggling with her back against Garret Raymond, who had one hand clamped over her mouth!

He smiled, his gray eyes sparkling, and released Arlene with an amused, "Hi." He looked with appreciation at Piper's exposed breasts.

She gasped, "Garret? You came to see me?" Then she squeaked as she realized how much of her could be seen and, scrambling, turned her back, grabbed up a towel, and clamped it to her chest in an agony of embarrassment.

Arlene said cheerfully, "I'm sorry. I was trying to warn you, but he wouldn't let me." She bent down and put the lotion next to Piper's towels.

In hollow, measured tones Piper forced herself to inquire: "How much did you hear?" She ignored what he'd seen by closing her mind to it.

13

Before Arlene could answer, Garret replied smoothly, "That you need to save someone from Barb Tallman."

Still with her back to them, Piper probed, "Arlene?"

"He followed me down when I came to tell you he was here."

"I think I'll drown myself." Piper considered that.

"If you did, how could you take me to lunch or save whoever it is from Barb Tallman?" Garrett asked reasonably.

"There is that," she agreed slowly, as if debating how important that was, under the circumstances. She peeked over her bare shoulder to see that Arlene was leaving, and Garret was peeling off his shirt. "Arlene?" she called after her sister, who was deserting her.

"He gave me a dollar to move his car into the shade," she explained airily as she vanished.

"Shade . . ." she cautioned as her eyes turned to a bemused Garret, ". . . is close to trees. You've never seen Arlene drive."

He threw down his shirt and stuck his fingers into his ears. "Tell me when it's over," he instructed as he squinted and pretended to brace himself for the sound of the crash.

That made her giggle, and he grinned back at her, removed his fingers from his ears, and looked around the river, up at the trees hanging over it, at the rope attached to one of them to swing over the water, and at the marvel of the private cove. "This is just great." He sat down carefully, undid his sneakers, and put them aside, then he took a towel and spread it on his side of the pier. He picked up the radio, arbitrarily changed the station, and lay down, saying, "Be a darling and rub some lotion on me, would you?" He licked a smile from his lips and added, ". . . and I'll do the same for you."

14

They heard the car motor roar to life and both froze. It revved, throbbing and roaring, then settled into a purr. Their eyes met and clung, his terribly amused, until the motor was turned off. No crash. He pretended to collapse with relief, making her laugh.

His body was gorgeously tanned and he didn't need any suntan lotion. Very self-consciously Piper moved onto her knees to his side. She wanted the excuse to touch him, so she put lotion on his back, with one hand holding the towel clamped to her. She felt so strange she thought she might have the beginnings of sunstroke. She'd never had sunstroke, and she wasn't sure of the symptoms. She'd never been aroused by a man, so she didn't know those symptoms either. Finished, she set the timer and feeling weird, she lay down on her stomach a little way from him, with the towel carefully under her chest.

Quite willingly he sat up and gently and very thoroughly smoothed lotion on her back and sides. His stroking was sensuous, smooth, and subtle, but since she'd held her arms close to her body, he didn't do the sides of her breasts.

His hand on her bare back had caused the strange symptoms to increase and she was a little dizzy. She suspected it wasn't the sun, but Garret, and she became a little breathless. She peeked at him as he lay back down on his stomach, his face toward her, his eyes closed. He was devastatingly handsome. His blond hair was sun-bleached on the surface but underneath it was a darkened gold. She couldn't believe he was real and was actually there with her. If she kissed him, would he turn into a frog? He had to be magic. Then she thought about kissing his mouth.

He opened his eyes and caught her looking at him in that way, and he smiled as if he knew what she was

15

thinking. She closed her eyes tightly. There was only silence, then she peeked, and he laughed out loud, and he thought how young she was. Too young. A good kid, but impossibly young.

He gave a wide yawn and after that they were quiet. There was a faint breeze, the river's current rocked the pier gently, and she heard his breathing slow and deepen as he fell asleep. She wondered why he was so tired. How late had he been out last night? It was none of her business. With him asleep, she refastened her top.

When the timer rang an hour was up, and she turned over and put lotion on the front of her body. Then she wakened him. He rolled over lazily and suggested she put lotion on his chest. His voice was purring and sleepy, and a tingling sensation vibrated through her. She said primly that he was perfectly capable of doing that himself.

He reached for the lotion, then on impulse he leaned over it and kissed her lips very softly. Her eyes flew open wide and she was still. He raised himself up enough to look at her and thought again how very young she was.

She saw that he had tiny laugh lines at the corners of his eyes and faint creases beside his mouth where he smiled. How old was he? she wondered, suddenly feeling out of her depth. He was so different from the guys she knew. He even walked differently—with a confidence they didn't have. Was he twenty-four? Or maybe even twenty-five? She waited for him to kiss her again.

However, Garret slowly retreated to his own towel. She was so annoyed with him then that she put the straw hat over her face and lay under it, frowning. She moved restlessly.

Watching her, Garret was disturbed and he became restless. Finally he said, "Let's go eat."

16

She said they had sunned the front of their bodies for only ten minutes. He said she could do that tomorrow. She replied it was going to rain tomorrow. Then she put the hat back over her face and lay still.

He wondered if she knew how seductive she was as she lay there. He wasn't sure. She appeared so guileless. If it had been Barb, he'd know it was calculated. As Piper sighed impatiently and fidgeted, his eyes raked her body. She lay straight, her hands beside her thighs, palms down, her legs straight, her heels only about five inches apart, but her toes were straight up, showing her tension. Was she posing?

The curves of her breasts were visible at the sides of her top as she shifted her body. Lying there, she looked ready to receive a man. His body stirred at the thought. He looked away and stared off down the river. "I think we should go have lunch; I'm hungry."

If she'd been more sophisticated, she'd have understood, but she didn't. She agreed, loaded him down with all the paraphernalia, and chattered along as she laughed at his pretense to falter going up the bank.

After she'd changed they went out to his dark green Porsche. He held the door for her and she slid in quickly. When he got in the other side and was putting the key in the ignition, she commented coolly, "Nice."

He smiled with a quick glance at her and asked where they should go. She suggested getting hamburgers and perhaps going somewhere in the country for a picnic. And she raised her eyebrows in a casual way.

He nodded, slid dark glasses over his eyes thus covering their amusement, and followed her directions to find the hamburgers.

"Are you around long?" She thought that sounded very mature.

"No. I just dropped by this morning to see if you'd like to have a brief affair."

She couldn't believe he'd said that. Her head whipped around and her lips parted in shock, but she felt the flood-tide of a wild sensation through her body. She blushed and was breathing through her mouth again.

His face was expressionless as he skillfully negotiated the narrow winding road. He had to be kidding. "Well . . ." she began. Two could play at that game. "I wouldn't be unwilling . . ." Her face flushed scarlet. It was one thing to play at being mature and worldly, but quite another to handle it well.

"Good," he said, as if that settled that.

"But . . ."

"Some problem?" he asked with polite inquiry.

"You see, Mother said if I ever did, she'd gather all the women around and I'd be stoned to death. And then Dad would kill the guy, cutting him precisely across the middle with a gatling gun. That makes it a terrible burden on . . . one. If you like the guy . . . the man . . . enough to, well, if you should like him *enough,* you'd hate for all that to happen."

"Yes," he replied judiciously. "I could see that would cause one to hesitate." They drove for a while. "So you're a virgin?"

"Obviously."

"Obviously?" His voice was somewhat unsteady with humor.

"Well, if I wasn't, I'd be under a pile of rocks, Dad would be waiting on death row, and he, whoever he was, would be lying in his grave, neatly sliced in two."

18

"Of course. I should have realized that." He nodded agreeably. "But they'd never have managed to get the smile off his face."

Her cheeks flooded with color, but she was pleased too. How romantic he was. "Do you play a saxophone?" she inquired dreamily.

"No," he replied. "But I can play *Chopsticks* on the piano."

"Oh." Her tone was a little flat.

"*Chopsticks* doesn't make it with you?"

"Saxophones turn me on." She went scarlet again with the silly misused phrase.

"*Do* they now?" He gave her an interested glance.

They drove into the carry-out lane at the hamburger stand and as he eased up to give their order he inquired with courtesy, "What do virgins eat?"

She rewarded that with a frigid glance and replied, "Keep that up and you'll have a knuckle sandwich," and immediately wished she'd bitten her tongue. That's what came of being the oldest and always around younger, immature siblings. She hurried to say she wanted the usual, burger, fries, and a Coke, before she turned and looked out of her window with what she hoped was cool indifference.

They drove to Route 97 and eventually ended up near the tiny community of Rock Creek and located a rocky creek. It was isolated, the water was clear over the rocks, and the place they'd discovered was very pretty. As they ate their picnic Piper found he worked for the government in some kind of electronics, or computers, or something like that.

Being established in business made him seem very old,

19

and it made her sad. The oldest of her acquaintances was the Simpson boy, who graduated from West Point in June.

Trying to entertain him, she made him wade in the little rock-bottomed creek. Although he didn't really want to, he was agreeable. Then she found he could skip stones on the water's surface and he showed off nicely, doing that. She maneuvered him into kissing her, which he did even nicer, but he seemed withdrawn from her. He asked if she was going on to college and what courses she'd be taking.

"Since Mother teaches, that's what my parents think I should do."

"What do you want to do?" He was somewhat indifferent and seemed only to be filling silence as he skipped another stone.

"Well. I do like to draw."

"Why not do that?" he asked.

"Not very many artists make any kind of a living."

"It won't matter; you'll marry," he predicted.

"Not necessarily . . ."

He laughed a snort of disbelief. "Oh, baby, you'll not escape for long." And he leaned to find another stone.

After a pause she asked, "Have you seen any of the places around? Like New Salem State Park, or Lincoln's home in Springfield?"

Lying, he shook his head, his eyes meeting hers as if he were losing a debate with himself. Then, almost with reluctance, he asked, "Would you like to show me around tomorrow?"

Her breath caught as she exclaimed, "Oh, yes!" and she beamed and her eyes sparkled.

Inwardly he groaned. What had made him say that? She was a child. A sexy-bodied, marvelously made, beautiful child. He really should back off, for her sake. But he hadn't realized that it was already too late for him.

It rained the next day as Piper had predicted. They didn't even notice. Her shirt matched the blue in the plaid of her cotton slacks and the color made her eyes into pools for a man to drown in.

They trooped through the Capitol building, and went to Lincoln's home to look into each room. The donated or loaned furniture was from the Lincoln era. Piper told Garret the only difference between the Morling home and Lincoln's was the Morling plumbing was marginally better.

He wasn't conscious of how often his eyes were on her, but she knew, and she reacted by being very animated, laughing and flirting with him. He was playing with fire, and so was she.

They parked on the way to New Salem, eating another picnic lunch, that time inside the rain-drenched car. Piper thought it very cozy, but he thought it was too close, and he wanted her so badly that he was uncomfortable.

When she'd finished eating, she discreetly licked her lips, but before she could wipe them with her napkin, he stopped her hands with one of his and, with his other, turned her head and held it while he thoroughly kissed her. He'd meant to do less than that; but she began to tremble as her lips slowly parted, and she kissed him back.

He groaned against her mouth, gathered her across the space separating them, and crushed her to him, his hands hard along the paths he'd longed to touch, his mouth hungry for her as he kissed her on her throat, breathing into her the hollow of her neck, his tongue licking along her ear. Then, with great effort, he stopped himself, sat her back on her side of the car, and told her, quite seriously, that she must behave or he couldn't be responsible for what happened.

That startled her. "What did I do?"

With a mock frown he growled, "You licked your lips in a particularly sensuously tempting manner."

Incredulous, she burst out laughing. "Licked my lips?"

"Yes," he replied, keeping his face perfectly serious.

"How could that . . . ?"

"It does, believe me. Don't do it again." Then, as an afterthought, he instructed, "Unless I tell you to."

"Men are strange."

He growled again. "Only because we're hobbled by civilization." And he ran rough hands through his blond hair, tumbling it very attractively.

"Oh!" she gasped dramatically. "Oh! That drives me wild when you mess up your hair that way!" And her laughter skipped along the teasing words. She grabbed him and started to give him a quick kiss, but his arms wrapped around her, and he shifted her effortlessly in that confined space until she was lying across his chest, her breasts squashed against his hard body. She quit laughing as his hands prowled restlessly over her back. He looked down at her, then he leaned slowly toward her as his hands lifted her to meet his hungry mouth.

She didn't make even a token attempt to escape. Her lips parted and she gave a little moan just before his mouth claimed hers. In sensual timelessness they kissed, almost as if it were a formal mouth-dance. Their heads slowly turned; their pivot was their mouths and their tongues.

Piper had never been kissed like this. She knew as sure as she was lying there in his arms that she must stop. Instead, she slid her hand up his chest and boldly curled it around the nape of his neck, pressing his head closer to her, awakened by a torrent of sensations new to her and very awesome in their power.

When he lifted his mouth she lay lax and pale, almost feeling faint and on the verge of tears. She didn't really understand the odd sensations, but she didn't want him to let her go.

Abruptly he said, "Sit up!"

She could hardly coordinate her movements. He helped her with rather harsh hands. She frowned and began to protest, but he opened his door and slid out into the steadily falling rain.

She looked around to see if someone was coming as she tried to stuff her blouse into her slacks and straighten herself, but her hands were languid, her mind bemused, and she couldn't see clearly through the rain-splattered windows.

After a time he came back, took a T-shirt from the front storage of the Porsche tossed it onto the front seat and swung his wet shirt into the backseat. He settled into the car, rubbed his dripping hair with a handkerchief, and pulled on the dry T-shirt. Then, still not speaking, he put the key into the ignition, pulled back onto the highway, and headed through lessening rain for New Salem State Park, just outside Petersburg. She offered that Lincoln had surveyed the town of Petersburg. He made no reply.

She said, "My Dad earned a scout badge walking the Lincoln Trail from New Salem to Springfield. Lincoln had walked it. He had to wear his bedroom slippers to church the next day, his feet were so swollen."

"Lincoln's?" He wasn't really listening.

"No. My Dad's."

She had no idea what was wrong or why the tension

between them had become a wall. Why should he be angry?

He followed the markers and they drove up the hill into the park. Perfunctorily he read the signs and they looked into the cabins. She'd seen the village so many times before that her mind was free to wonder about Garret's conduct. It didn't help.

After a while he stopped reading the sign on how to make soap and stood frowning down at her with troubled eyes. "I'm twenty-eight," he snapped.

She drew a surprised breath. Twenty-eight! She'd thought he'd be twenty-five at the very most. *Twenty-eight!* And she turned away, head down, and started to walk aimlessly. He caught up with her. "I'm too old for you." And sadly, she nodded. For some reason that offended him, and he heard himself saying, "That's only ten years." But she just heaved a long melancholy sigh.

Then he thought: If it made her unhappy, she must have some feelings for him. His heart lifted and feeling a little more cheerful he began to tease her. "I would say—just off-hand, you understand—that there is something of an attraction between us."

She raised mournful eyes and saw that he was being humorous and she frowned. "Something of an attraction?"

"Yes. So we have to take it easy or this thing could get entirely out of hand," he instructed. "And while I'm perfectly willing to accept your virginity, I am somewhat deterred by the thought of the gatling gun." She nodded slowly, as if she could see his point quite well.

He continued in his instructor's role. "I'm not going to be around this area for very long. Just until my great-aunt Miriam's estate is settled, and I'm not the marrying kind.

24

I do enjoy your company, and I must say that looking at you is a special pleasure, but we're going to have to space kisses, and you have to keep your hands off me altogether."

"*My* hands!" she sputtered with fine indignation. "What about *your* greedy paws?"

He considered her complaint. "Well, I think if you behave more properly, I can manage me." And he smiled.

"Me!" She was getting huffy. "If *I* . . . !"

"I'll help," he reassured her, but spoiled it by leaning over and kissing her open, protesting mouth. "But you can't get indignant, because it arouses me." And he grinned, teasing her.

She inhaled quickly to yell at him, but he held up an admonishing finger and cautioned, "You're being very exciting." He kissed her again, then turned away, he informed her, to avoid being tempted by her stormy looks and flashing blue eyes.

She stood there, trying to think of an answer, then grated, "I'm trying to think of a way to kick you without getting mud on your trousers."

"Consideration is very provocative," he counseled as he turned back toward her.

"Oh, for Pete's sake!"

"So is exasperation." He raised his brows, half-closed his eyes, and nodded, agreeing with his own words. He reached for her, but she turned and ran back down the lane between the rebuilt cabins to his car in the parking lot.

On the way back to her house she would hardly reply to his offerings of conversation but as they turned into the road that led to the Morling lane he asked, "Could you come to dinner with me and then we could go to that new

25

film on reincarnation everyone's talking about? Have you seen it?"

"No."

"Would you like to? With me?" He looked at her.

"Y-yes," she replied woefully.

He eased to a halt at her gate. "How about seven? I understand there's a new restaurant this side of Springfield that's very good. How about that?"

"Okay. I'll be ready at seven." Then automatically she told him, "I had a nice time. Thank you."

Very gravely he replied, "You're welcome. I'll see you at seven."

When she opened the front door, her mother was there. "He didn't even walk you to the door," she accused.

Piper nodded without much spirit. "We're going to dinner and then to the film *Again.*"

"Again? Just what's that about?" Mrs. Morling demanded suspiciously.

Piper sighed, "Reincarnation."

And the sound of the sigh was such that it caused her mother to frown and narrow her eyes as she weighed Piper's mood.

When Garret called for Piper at seven, her father met him. Mr. Morling was distantly courteous, asking questions that appeared mild but which were sharp and probing. Piper squirmed. Garret was politely responsive, replying with candor.

It seemed to Piper her parents were very cold and unfriendly, and that their questions were uncalled for. Who was his family? Where did he work? How long had he been there? What were his political affiliations? Whether Garret was really Republican or just astutely attuned to the farm belt of the Midwest, Piper didn't know.

After an interminable time, they escaped, and Piper was in an agony of divided emotions: wanting to apologize for her parents' interrogation, and loyally not wanting to make apologies. So she was silent.

Piper was resigned to the evening being a disaster. They barely spoke all through what was a delicious dinner. Then leaving the restaurant, they ran into Barb Tallman and two other women, who were just entering. It might not have been so bad if Barb had had a date, but she did not and seeing Piper with Garret must have been too much.

Barb brushed against Garret as she took his arm and said with a feline purr, "What are you doing, Garret, baby-sitting?"

He disengaged his arm from her hands as he said they'd been enjoying a good chat. He smiled at Piper, took her arm, and walked her away.

Piper was suffused with embarrassment. How kind Garret was to say he'd enjoyed her conversation when they'd barely spoken. So when they were out of earshot, she said, "Look, we don't have to go to the film. You could just take me on home."

"Oh, don't you feel well?"

"Uh . . . no." Then more positively, she said, "No. I don't at all."

"How about some aspirin?" he suggested. "Since her claws didn't touch you, you won't get cat-scratch fever. It's probably just allergy to her dander. If we park a block or so away from the theater, and you take deep breaths, you should get her out of your system. Anyway, the picture might be scary and someone has to be there to hold my hand."

He watched as the laugh bubbled up from her toes. She was an absolute delight. She'd settle back to giggles, then the laugh would erupt again, and soon they were both helpless with laughter. When she caught her breath, she scolded, "You're a complete idiot."

Standing there on the street, with people glancing their way, he kissed her and he told her he always kissed blue-eyed brunettes who called him an idiot. It was a compulsion he'd inherited, genetically, from a great-great-great-great-great uncle who *had* been an idiot and whose romantic attention was captured by women saying the word. It was something about their mouths, the opening of the lips that set him afire . . . and that's the part he'd inherited.

The movie was really quite good. Afterward they went for coffee and discussed whether or not they believed in reincarnation. They decided there just might be something to it. Piper said she thought he'd been a barbarian. He pretended offense and asked why on earth she thought that? She said because he'd complained about the hobbles of civilization.

The next morning after breakfast her mother told Piper sternly that Mrs. White had called and her sister had it from her cousin that Piper had been seen standing on the street in Springfield kissing that Raymond man in public!

"Oh, she's mistaken. I had a gnat in my eye." She returned her mother's look quite steadily.

But her mother wasn't fooled. "He's too old for you, Piper. I don't believe you should go out with him again."

"He won't be here for very long."

Mrs. Morling questioned her keenly. "I thought he was going with the Tallman girl."

"Wherever did you hear that?" Piper appeared surprised.

"Her mother told Mrs. Lee that she was surprised you'd interfere in Barb's life that way . . . so deliberately."

Piper looked her mother in the eye and observed, "You can't steal what doesn't want taking."

"That the burglar's hymn?"

Not long after that Garret came by, tooted his car horn as he swung into the lane, and got out to grin at Piper as she came to the gate. Then his eyes went past her, stopping his impulse to give her a quick kiss, for there on the porch was her mother. He pushed his sunglasses up on his forehead and greeted Mrs. Morling. She nodded in reply, but her lips were set in a firm line.

"Let's go," he said to Piper.

So she called, "I'll be back soon, Mother."

"I'll be practicing my aim," her mother replied meaningfully.

Garret was hit by such a spasm of racking coughs that Piper pounded his back. Alarmed by his sudden choking, she bent to peer anxiously at his face and found his eyes brimming with hilarity. The coughs were to cover his laughter. She whacked him a good one.

After they'd driven away, Piper said her mother wanted to know what they talked about. He grinned at her and asked didn't she think they talked or did she think he only practiced his wiles on her? Piper suspected the latter.

He pulled to the side of the road and reached for her. But she gasped, alarmed, and said, "For Pete's sake, Garret, don't stop here! Mrs. Lee lives in that house right over there and she watches everything like a hawk with army field glasses! And she's a friend of Mrs. Tallman's."

Garret burst out laughing. "The CIA." But he restarted the motor, and he turned back onto the highway.

"You mean spies?"

He grinned. "Undercover agents."

"Nothing is undercover here, believe me," she informed him fervently. "And being the oldest is a real pain. You have to be the one to break in the parents all by yourself."

"Why couldn't you be old enough to have an apartment?" he wanted to know. "I could move in for a while, and no one would know."

"Someone would," she was positive. "You wouldn't believe how small the world is."

"Why *don't* you have an apartment? Where will you live at college?"

"With my aunt."

"Part of the espionage system," he guessed.

"Probably. I don't know her very well. Her name's Emily Morling, and she's a law professor at Illinois. She lives just off campus. Been there a hundred years. I only remember her expression when we called her Auntie Em the way Dorothy did in *The Wizard of Oz*. She wasn't terribly amused."

"You ought to be in a sorority."

"This won't cost anything," she explained.

"Well, there's something to be said for that. Where can we go to park? I want to muss up your hair and flush your cheeks with my whiskers and wrestle with you."

She grinned. "Actually there isn't anywhere close. This sassy little car is a dead giveaway. Everyone in the territory knows it by now. Also why you're here, that you've dated that Tallman woman, and that you've been seen kissing me on the street in Springfield last night. I told mother I had a gnat in my eye."

He was amazed. "Someone called her?"

"Mrs. White, whose sister's cousin saw us."

"I don't believe this!" He shook his head. "Now I know why my grandparents left this area."

Taking a guess, she suggested, "They were wicked and did disgraceful things they wanted to keep secret."

"Probably. Like trying to seduce nice boys and girls on the streets of Springfield by kissing them lasciviously."

"Garret!" she protested, but her eyes sparkled.

"Are we far enough past Mrs. Lee's house?"

"Yes. But that's my cousin's house over there. And that one belongs to one of the women in Mother's bridge club. And . . ."

"My God! How does any courting get done around here?"

She shook her head. "It never does. We stick a pin in a list of names, get married, and *then* find out what it's all about."

He said that seemed a chancy way to go about it, and she agreed. He said there was a dance on the pier where they'd met and why didn't they go that night? She wanted to know if there wasn't some other place they could go and just dance and not have to be with everyone else. Again he thought how young she was. So eager to be alone with him and so blatant about it. Not blatant in a flirtatious way, but artlessly. He had to be careful for her sake, but he looked at her, sitting beside him in his car, and he liked it that she was there.

CHAPTER TWO

Mostly saddled with her brothers' and sisters' company, they spent several days swimming in the river and playing violent croquet on the front lawn. Jennifer was a terror and the quiet Paul was surprisingly aggressive.

But occasionally Piper and Garret escaped their chaperons and walked alone, hand in hand, down the riverway, kissing often, Garret driven to the brink of losing control and leaving her enthralled. Their courtship was brief, intense, sensual, and not very smooth.

Then he came for her one evening to go to Havana, located on the Illinois River about forty miles from Springfield. He had on a blue sport jacket, tie, and slacks with a wheat-colored shirt. He looked wonderful with the colors accenting his blond hair.

They were going to Havana for a dinner of channel catfish. She looked like a ray of sunshine in buttercup yellow, and he watched with appreciation as she swung her nice legs into his car.

As they drove from the lane onto the paved road, Garret asked her, "Do you get the impression that your parents are rather hostile toward me?"

If he'd been looking for sympathy, he'd come to the

wrong girl. "If you think they're hostile to you, you should see how they are to me!"

"Oh?" he inquired. "What's the trouble?"

"You!"

He exclaimed indignantly, "What's wrong with me?"

"They think you're too old, too sophisticated, and that you're toying with me."

He could agree to that. "I'd sure as hell like to."

"No way."

"You have a closed mind," he complained.

"I have a vivid picture of being stoned and you being cut in two . . ."

Impatiently he supplied the rest, ". . . by a gatling gun." Then he added, "They wouldn't really, you know."

"I can see why you wouldn't mind risking it. It's okay for you. I'd think a gatling gun would be a whole lot quicker than rocks, for Pete's sake!"

"Do you know how often you say 'for Pete's sake'?"

"Yes. I know. But Mother gets so tense over the words I choose."

"Your parents have a lot to say in your life, don't they?"

"Why not?" she asked.

"Why should they?"

"Well . . ." She hesitated, then she said slowly, "I wish I could say this exactly right. I don't think they interfere the way you imply. When they met and fell in love they didn't just hop into bed together. They were committed to each other, and they accepted it . . . the responsibility. They've worked hard to have us, and take care of us, and I know there were times when my mother especially would have liked to run off and been a beachcomber or run in the woods with the satyrs. She's a dreadful romantic."

"You're kidding," he teased her.

"Honest."

"She hides it well."

Piper missed the drollness. "It must make it even harder for her when a godlike man comes along and bedazzles her daughter and wants only a temporary dalliance, because she has to fight not only him, but her own empathy."

"Do I bedazzle you?"

She gave him a wicked look. "So you instantly recognized yourself as godlike?"

His laughter erupted, and after the first gust of it, he cast a satyrlike glance at her. She was watching him with brimming humor and, he thought, she was glorious. "Baby, as my great-aunt Miriam always said, 'You are a stitch!' "

"What was she like?"

"Old."

"Why did she choose you as executor?"

"Other than my many sterling qualities, too numerous to mention, she loved me. I seem to attract the devotion of old ladies." He'd been half-bantering but, considering her question, his face became thoughtful as he watched the road lit by his headlights winding ahead of them. "I wish I'd been old enough to have known her. She was something of a rebel. She'd worked hard for women's right to vote and she would have been in the forefront with the ERA if she'd been stronger.

"She had rather violent opinions about the women who opposed it. Except for one voluptuous blonde in California, whose picture was in the paper as having left the kiddies home with their daddy while she went traveling to *oppose* women's liberation! That made my aunt slap her bony old knee and guffaw." He slowed, sat up straighter, slowed more. "Ah, here we are."

34

He shifted down and turned onto a rocky, potholed lane, easing the car carefully. Then he swung onto an abandoned farmer's cul-de-sac. "I scouted this out after I left you this afternoon." He turned the wheel and nosed the car so that it was pointed toward the lane, then he doused the lights, pushed his seat back, and shrugged out of his jacket.

"Now, Garret . . ." Her eyes were blinded by the temporary total darkness.

"Oh, by the way, here."

As her eyes adjusted to the darkness, she saw he was holding out a piece of white paper toward her. "What's this?" she asked.

He had twisted around to lay his coat on the small back seat. "That's the list of things we discussed tonight," he explained. "You know, to tell your mother when she asks."

Piper opened the glove compartment to read by that light, but the sounds he was making caused her to look at Garret. He'd loosened his tie and was unbuttoning his shirt.

She asked sharply, "What are you doing?"

"I'm getting ready to kiss you."

With growing alarm she questioned him. "And you have to unbutton your shirt to kiss me?"

"It's a fitted shirt."

"What's that got to do with it?" She was sneaking little peeks around into the dark beyond the car.

He replied reasonably, "The shirt restricts how deeply I can breathe. I'm fixing it so I don't have to stop to breathe while I'm kissing you. See?"

"That great-uncle who was an idiot . . ."

"Remarkable man. You should read his diaries. Even

35

Penthouse won't touch them." He'd undone his cuffs, rested one wrist on the steering wheel, and held out the other hand to her. "Come here," he said casually.

The reasonableness of his tone rather disconcerted her because it sounded so logical, but the open shirt cautioned her. Quickly she bent her head back over the list. "I have to read what we're talking about."

"Read over my shoulder," he said, then he reached over and, again, effortlessly, he maneuvered her so that she was turned, lying across his chest, facing him.

With their noses close, she observed, "You're very good at this. You must have had a lot of practice."

"I had a large stubborn dog." He bent his head and kissed her.

There was silence. When he lifted his head, she accused him, "You breathe while you're kissing."

"That's just surface breathing—to keep my nose going."

"Garret . . ."

"Read the list. I'll find something to do to entertain myself while you're ignoring me." He smiled politely, but his eyes gleamed. "In order to read over my shoulder, you have to put your arms around my neck." His lips quirked.

"Just one arm." She curled one arm up to lie between her breasts while she put the other up around his head and adjusted her body so she could read from the list: "How the Red Sox are doing: poorly. That the corn is looking good . . . ?"

He laughed, hugged her closely, arm and all, and kissed her again.

"If you're going to kiss me," she protested crossly, "move your head that way. I can't see if you block the light."

36

But he put his head down the side of her face and blew into her neck, moving his face along her cheek and nibbling her ear with his open mouth and darting tongue.

She gasped and involuntarily her body moved sensuously. But when she heard his smug sound in response, she asked incredulously, "The Dow-Jones averages?"

With his mouth still where her throat and shoulder met, he murmured, "That shows how unemotional and practical our conversation was."

She gasped, "You're incredible!"

He moaned in agreement and claimed her mouth. When he released it, her head went back and her breath was almost labored from the tide of emotion and the demands of her throbbing, inflamed blood. In a subtle purr, Garret said, "See? Your shirt's too tight." And before she knew what he was doing, he'd unbuttoned it, her bra was around her neck, and her cool, bare breasts were pressed against his warm chest!

A vibrant rush of emotion swept over the surface of her body as her tender nipples were teased by the crisp hair of his chest. All the alarm bells started clanging in her head, and a kaleidoscope of warnings, advice, and finger-shakings whirled before her closed eyes.

She felt his body shift and his mouth move down her chest and softly over her nipple. Her toes curled, her lips parted, and hot sensual feelings licked through her body. Nobody had ever told her it would be like this.

She lay in his arms, her hands petting his chest, ruffling the curly hairs, taking pleasure in the feeling. She felt the marvelous strength of his throat and face and went on to run her fingers along his head, burying them in his thick blond hair, which was damp with sweat.

His mouth was greedy and his hands hard and intense.

37

His breath was warm, and it astonished her that he was breathing as if he'd been running.

Piper became more languid, awash with a pleasure that was not yet urgent. She had turned a deaf ear to the clamoring warnings, and she stretched enticingly, encouraging him, but she was scarlet-faced because she knew she should not be doing it.

He pulled back to look at her. Her eyes had deepened with desire to a dark blue. Soft and inviting, her mouth was waiting for his. His eyes glittered over her bare loveliness. He expelled a steam blast of air and complained, "It'd be nice if you'd resist a little."

That surprised her. She tried to think why he'd want her to do that? "To make it more . . . exciting for you?"

"No! To *stop* me!"

That confused her. "Stop you?"

"Don't you know what you're doing to me? Look, baby, I'd no intention of making love to you. But if you don't give me a little opposition, I sure as hell will!"

"Oh . . ." Her tears started. "You . . . don't . . . want . . ."

"Oh, baby," he groaned, and put his head down and slowly rubbed his sweaty face over her sweet naked breasts. In a kind of despair he added, "I feel as if I've contacted a fatal disease and you're the only cure." His husky voice broke on the word. He lifted his head again to look at her flooded eyes. "I don't want to get married."

She gulped. "Me either."

"You don't?" He couldn't believe she'd said that.

"I'm too young." She sniffled.

"Oh, Piper, baby . . ." He lifted her up against him to cradle her gently, hushing her tears. "If only we could just have an affair . . ."

She took a breath to speak.

But grimly he interrupted. "I know, your mother'd send out for the rock-throwers, and your father would man the gatling gun."

"We'll just . . . have to . . ."

He nodded and finished it for her. ". . . quit seeing each other."

She cried. He kissed her forehead. She sat up and he helped fasten her bra and straighten her shirt. They got out of the car on either side, tucked in their shirts, smoothed their clothes, and she combed her hair. They got back into the car, he started it, shifted, and eased onto the rocky lane, but before he'd turned toward Havana she said she wasn't hungry and she'd better just go on home.

They were mostly silent after that. She said once that she'd enjoyed knowing him, and she wished she was older and hadn't been raised so strictly. He grunted. She knew that her upbringing had not stopped them from making love. It had been Garret.

As her sad eyes studied his face, as if to memorize every line, every feature, she blurted, "Are you going back to that Tallman woman?" She could have bitten off her stupid tongue.

Things were too grim for that to be funny. He turned a bleak look toward her and met her eyes, bright with brimming tears. He groaned, "Oh, baby . . ." and pulled off the road. They came together in wordless sounds and moans of misery.

All the arguments they gave each other were exactly right. And each agreed with the other: They would be foolish to see each other again. One couldn't argue with logic.

He drove her home, walked her to the door, and gave

her an extremely tender, chaste, farewell kiss. She was trembling and unsteady. He left her there and got into his car and drove away. She watched the taillights disappear and knew she would never see him again and how on earth did God expect her to live out the rest of her life without him?

She wobbled into the house. And there was her mother. She'd not just left the light on as she always did, but this time she was sitting up, waiting for Piper, an indication of her unease.

Mrs. Morling's voice was brusque. "Are you all right?"

"Oh, Mother . . ." Piper burst into tears.

"What happened?" Mrs. Morling snapped.

"We're never going to see each other again."

"Oh?" Mrs. Morling gasped with unconcealed relief, and took her bawling daughter into her arms.

The next morning when Mrs. Morling went to get the paper from the tube by the mailbox, there was Garret sitting in his car by the gate. He was still wearing the clothes he'd worn the night before, and he needed a shave.

Unsmiling, Mrs. Morling said an unbending, scant, "Good morning," as if, with that, he'd go away.

He opened the door and tiredly got out of his car. He looked so wretched that sympathy nudged her. He ran a hand over his already abused hair and began, "Uh . . ." and looked at her.

She'd had a dog once that could look that way, and it had been a pain because she couldn't refuse it anything and it'd never been properly trained because of that. She stiffened.

He looked up at the house then back to Mrs. Morling. "I wondered . . . is Piper . . . up?"

"I believe so." Piper was probably glued to the window, watching, but Mrs. Morling didn't call to her.

"Could . . . could I see her?" he asked reluctantly, as if he were being driven to it.

"Garret, I honestly don't believe . . ." she began determinedly but was interrupted by the banging of the screen door.

Her youngest, Robert, came cheerfully bouncing down the steps shouting, "Garret! After breakfast do I get to ride in your car?"

After that everything got out of control. One of the problems with being hospitable, Mrs. Morling thought, is that your children become infected with it, but they have no discernment, and you end up feeding and harboring all sorts of people and animals.

Garret stayed for breakfast.

Surprisingly, Arlene was insensitive to the tension. It was fourteen-year-old Jennifer whose instinct picked up on it. But instead of being uncomfortable or sympathetic, she was excessively interested and studied Piper and Garrett avidly.

As always with the Morling family, everyone talked, and Mrs. Morling had the executive ability of keeping track of several things at a time. Besides the actual cooking and serving of food, she noted the intense awareness between Piper and Garret and their quick glances at each other, the poignant catches when their eyes met, and their distracted monosyllabic replies to questions.

Mrs. Morling too saw Jennifer's captured attention and noted Arlene's indifference. It seemed to her that Paul didn't feel very well, although he was eating his share of the palm-sized pancakes. Robert was excited over the anticipated ride in Garret's Porsche. He knew everything

41

about it and the information flowed from him; he kept telling Arlene and Jennifer that it would be a ride they'd never forget.

Poor Piper. She wasn't eating. But, then, Garret was only drinking coffee and he looked terrible. Mrs. Morling wondered if he'd slept at all. Lord knows what would happen to them. Here they'd known each other less than two weeks and look at them! It would never do. Yet secretly she couldn't help being caught up in the romance of their unhappy situation.

Mrs. Morling suggested Paul take a book down to the pier and fish for the day. He gave her a little smile, but hesitated over missing the car ride. Garret said he could go for a ride another day, and Paul gave him a bigger grin and disappeared.

After the plates were stacked in the dishwasher, Mrs. Morling sent the rest of the children outside. Garret adroitly lifted the top off his car, showing Robert exactly how it worked. Then he opened the back to show the boy the motor and listened to Robert expound on its merits.

There was room in the car only for the four of them. Quietly Piper said she'd wait on the porch. Garret's tired face had been very still as they'd exchanged a long look. Then he said it: "Wait for me," and that said everything. She slowly nodded.

When they returned, Piper stayed sitting on the porch swing. Arlene and Robert, chatting, moved around the porch for a while, then drifted away to chores or their own interests. Jennifer left reluctantly.

Wearily, Garret moved to the swing beside Piper. They sat for a long while not speaking, then he moved over a notch and lifted his arm around her, resting it on the back of the swing. She lay her head on his shoulder, as if that's

42

where it belonged. He bent his head and touched her lips with his. "What are we going to do?"

She shook her head hopelessly. "I don't know." She was too depressed even to care and her tears started again.

"Oh, baby . . ."

Inside, in the hall, Mrs. Morling stood quietly watching them across the living room, through the lace curtain that covered the front window, and her own eyes filled, but her mouth tightened with determination.

When Mr. Morling finished dinner that night, he agreed with his wife: It would not do. They told that to Piper, then to Garret, who listened, his head up, his jaw stubborn. Mr. Morling said the difference in their ages was such that they needed to back off from this attraction between them, and it would be better if they didn't see each other.

They suggested that Garret stay away from Piper until his vacation the next year. They could write and talk on the phone, but they shouldn't see each other. Garret was intelligent enough to realize how young Piper was, not only in years but in sophistication. All of it was unarguable. The young couple went out on the porch and talked for a long time and Piper cried some more.

It was midnight when her mother called softly, saying it was time to say good night. And again Piper watched the taillights until they faded from sight, and she went back to the swing. Her head throbbed and she sat in a miserable stupor.

After a while her mother came out to stand in the darkness of the porch. Finally she drew up a rocker and just sat, gently rocking but saying nothing.

"I'll never survive a year," said the voice from the swing.

"Oh, honey, you will," her mother reassured her.

"I don't see how."

"Wait and see how it goes. Come, darling, it's getting cool. Come to bed now."

"All right." Piper rose to her feet and looked down at her mother. "And thanks . . . for being around."

"Ahhhh." Mrs. Morling's voice was very unsteady.

Garret called Piper five times that next day, and the day after that, on the third call, Mrs. Morling said he really shouldn't talk to Piper that often. Garret agreed but asked to let them speak for just a minute. Reluctantly Mrs. Morling handed the phone to the hovering Piper.

He told her he'd been thinking of her and that he loved her. That made her weepy. He said a year wasn't that long, and she squeaked a doubtful agreement. He said he'd call that night, and she just bawled. Finally Jennifer took the phone from her weak hand, listened to the dial tone, and hung it up.

"Do you really love him?" Jennifer asked with clinical interest.

"I don't *know!*" Piper wailed.

"I should think you'd have some clue, carrying on as you are. You're being awfully dreary about everything."

"Go *away!*"

"I'm going. I'm going."

Piper dragged around, waiting for the phone to ring, not eating, being scolded for being so weepy, being told to straighten up and get her chores done, being told she was being far too dramatic, being told to drink some milk anyway, watching the clock until it was time she could take two more aspirin, and being reprimanded for that too.

Two long, miserable days limped by and the next was Garret's last day there. He would be going back to wherever it was he belonged, to do whatever it was he did.

His car drove into their lane just after supper. Robert came loping across the yard to the porch yelling, "He's back! He's back!"

The Morlings exchanged pained, anguished looks and went out on the porch. Garret had left his car, opened the gate, and was walking purposefully toward them when the screen door burst open, Piper erupting through it to hurl herself down the steps and into Garret's arms.

Garret clutched her fiercely to him and it was all so dramatic that it silenced the entire family, including the voluble Robert. Jennifer was fascinated, Arlene smiled and sighed, but Mrs. Morling's heart sank down to her shoes.

Mr. Morling cleared his throat. He was not untouched, and he said very kindly, "Well, Garret?"

"I'm taking her with me; we're going to be married."

"No," Mr. Morling denied in gentle opposition.

Piper had wrapped her arms around Garret's body and buried her face in his chest, weeping.

"For Pete's sake," Jennifer rolled her eyes to the sky in disgust. "All she does is cry!"

The dogs were bouncing around, the cats came to see what was going on, and Paul reminded his parents, "I didn't get my ride in his car yet." Arlene only hushed him absently. It was all awful.

Mr. Morling had said something about their not being sure enough to be married after such a brief acquaintance. He stressed that last word.

45

Garret argued that in five years everyone would realize they'd been right to marry; he knew it now, so did Piper. Piper? She cried.

They were all too emotionally involved for the debate to be brief. It was late when they convinced Garret he should go back to his motel; they'd see him in the morning.

And again on the porch, with Piper clinging to his body like a limpet, Garret moaned, "I feel as if I've been through a meat grinder." He hugged her, kissed her, then, peering into her face in the dark, he asked, "How could someone as beautiful as you cause so much trouble?"

"Me? Cause trouble?" she wailed. "Everything was fine until you came along!"

The next day the wedding was set for the third morning after that. Mrs. Morling's bridge club played Paul Revere spreading the news. Food and flowers were volunteered, people rallied around to help, and everything was done while Piper walked around in something of a daze, making Jennifer comment, "At least she's not crying!" And Arlene thought it all "romantic." "All romances have to have suffering," she philosophized.

Even while supervising everything, Mrs. Morling duly noted her daughters. Piper *had* seemed her most normal, and the cold-blooded Arlene was turning out to be the most bemused, amused romantic of them all, while Jennifer appeared coldly analytical! Children were strange, Mrs. Morling thought wryly.

Jennifer queried Garret, "What do you see in her? She does have a nice body, of course, that's built-in obsolescence, but besides the body, there's nothing!"

Garret was on his feet and not really hearing her had left the room, but Arlene gasped, "Why, Jennifer!"

Those next several days the house was like a busy airport and people trooped in and out, offering a wealth of conflicting suggestions. No one really thought they'd survive with their sanity intact.

Piper was a gorgeous bride. Her gown was her great-great-grandmother's. It was of a fine lawn, the skirt drawn into a subdued bustle. Its long sleeves and high neck were trimmed with dainty handmade lace, and there were forty tiny buttons from the high neck to the bottom of the tightly fitted overblouse and twenty buttons between the elbow and wrist of each sleeve.

Jennifer suggested, practically, to begin buttoning from the bottom. "Then if you missed one, it won't look so sloppy." And she decided when she married she too would use that dress. ". . . so don't wreck it," she had warned Piper. It was by far the least frilly and silly she'd ever seen.

Piper wore baby's-breath and violets in her hair, and Garret gave her his grandmother's diamond ring to wear with the circle of diamonds that was her wedding ring.

Her father solemnly gave her away, and by not blinking at all for the whole morning, her mother avoided tears slipping over and down her cheeks. At least, she thought, she hadn't blinked and that's why her eyes felt so strange.

The house and porches and yard were packed with guests. Garret's family had flown in, with bemused pleasure, and were overwhelmed with people trying to straighten them out on who was kin, friends, and strangers —that is, those who'd lived in the area only one generation.

Remarkably, Barb Tallman showed up with her family. She looked absolutely smashing in a lace gown that was

47

pale pink and stunning against her tanned skin. She stood in the receiving line and purred to Garret, "It's a mistake, you know. When you realize it, I'll be here." But Garret turned his head, so her kiss landed on his jaw. Piper missed the whole encounter.

She was in such a dream world that she was unaware of her parents' anguish. Their misty-eyed glances clung to her—their first little bird to leave their nest, and although their inquiries about Garret had revealed nothing untoward, they still had feelings of doubt about the marriage.

After the buffet lunch was demolished, Piper changed into her last year's two-piece summer suit and, amid rice and paper streamers, the newlyweds slipped into the dark green Porsche and, with calls and waves, drove away into the afternoon.

So when Mr. and Mrs. Garret Raymond arrived in St. Louis, it was only about three in the afternoon. They checked into a motel, carried their bags into their room, undressed, got into bed and, after a kiss or two, they went to sleep.

Garret had explained he was too tired to lift a finger, that they'd sleep an hour or so, take a swim, and after dinner he'd apply himself to overcoming his fear of gatling guns. He allowed himself one pat on her fanny, turned over, and went to sleep. She was grateful for the delay, as he'd suspected.

It was almost eight when they wakened. They exclaimed about that, for it gave them something easy to talk about. He had to get out of bed and take a cold shower, or they'd never get supper and take a swim, and she skinned into her bathing suit in such a hurry that she had to sit and wait for him.

They had the pool to themselves. They sent a waiter for champagne and a tray of hors d'oeuvres. They played and snacked and laughed and teased. When they went back to their room to change for dinner, Piper found that Garret had had a bottle of the champagne and another tray of appetizers and relishes delivered.

Garret said they had plenty of time before they had to eat. Perhaps after she got out of her wet suit, she'd be more comfortable in just a robe? Or she could just forget the robe altogether? She put on the robe. He wore a towel.

Then he sat her down on the side of the bed while he expertly opened the bottle. She asked him how he'd learned to do that so well. He said they'd had a sex education class in high school that demonstrated it. She laughed. He asked where did she think boys learned things? Then he smiled and asked, with exaggerated interest, did she know what else he'd learned in that class?

She blushed. He pretended shock and said her sex education classes must have been a lot more interesting than his! And he nodded his head in a slow, knowing way. His classes had been about the differences between the sexes.

"Oh, yes?" she had to inquire.

"Umm-hmm. About how women do the cooking and the men open champagne, and women mow the lawns and men lie in hammocks . . ."

She huffed protests, and he kissed her. Then, with an elaborate display of casualness, he produced a tape recorder, set it up like a magician setting up a special trick, inserted a cassette, set it to play, and bowed. And with insinuating sensualness the saxophone sound came on—a squealing, smoky sax, and accompanying it was a moody piano.

"Saxophones! I *love* saxophones!" Piper exclaimed.

"I know."

"How did you know that?"

"You said they turned you on. I'm not dumb, you know."

He fed her bits of hors d'oeuvres and had her sip the champagne and he kissed her a great deal. When he loosened her robe he told her it was so that she could breathe more easily, but he slid his hands inside and pulled her naked body to his as he dropped his towel. Then he laid her back and treasured her body and kissed her scarlet face as his hot hands caressed her. He probed and squeezed and kissed and suckled and licked and learned her until the room should have dripped from the steam, as they did.

She was surprised at the response her body made as he rubbed his whiskers gently into the backs of her knees, the insides of her elbows, and along the lobes of her ears. And he touched her in all her secret places, and his hot eyes watched her face as her lips parted, or her eyes closed, or were languidly opened, and he listened to her gasp or whisper his name, or moan, or almost purr.

And when, for a respite, he lay back on the pillows, she wouldn't leave him alone. She became bolder and leaned over him to stroke his chest, to kiss his mouth, and to touch his ear with her tongue. She didn't think doing it was nearly as exciting as having it done to her, but he apparently liked it. She leaned over him and moved her bare breasts on his hair rough chest, and he watched her avidly.

She slid down his steamy body to lick his nipple, then she moved up his slick body, liking the rough texture of him rubbing against her sensitive skin. She gently touched his mouth with hers, then darted her tongue out, as he'd done to her, and flicked it along his lip. It was an odd sensation to do that, and she felt bold.

She could have played with him for hours, but it was too much for him, and his already tense body went rigid. He took her into almost harsh arms to turn her, to ease onto her, and finally to take her with slow, hungry thrusts, running his hands over her love-drenched body. Her initial discomfort faded as she moved with a natural, easy rhythm, as if she had been making love to Garret all her life. But the feelings churning within her were unlike anything she had ever felt before. Garret was stirring her into a world where nothing was real except the feel of his body against hers, and the almost excruciatingly exquisite delight that her body was surrendering to.

When they lay spent, their breaths and heartbeats slowing in their still entwined bodies, they again became aware of the muted wailing of the sax. She chuckled in a low, intimate way that pleased him and she said, "You didn't need the saxophones. I haven't even heard them since you started the music."

In lazy indignation he protested, "You mean I wasted all that time and money—finding just the right songs?"

"No, not entirely." She petted his wet hair on the back of his head. "It made me realize that you fully intended to make love to me."

He gasped, "You hadn't had any clues to that before then?"

"No." She opened her eyes very wide to show her innocence.

"Why did you think I tried to strip and maul you every time I got you alone?"

She made a guess. "You were trying to attract my attention?"

He half-closed his eyes and smiled smugly. "I had your attention from the first minute you laid eyes on me."

She smiled in rueful agreement. "Did you know right away?"

"It was like I'd stuck my finger into a light socket."

"You've done that?"

"Inadvertently," he told her. "But when you finally relaxed against me while we danced, I knew I had to get you. I hadn't realized I'd have to go to such lengths, but I knew I had to have you."

She raised herself up to look at him more closely. "So that's really the only reason you married me?"

"Oh, no. Not entirely. I like the way you blush."

"I'm amazed at your good solid reasons for such a serious step," she clipped in a droll tone of voice.

"Your humor knocks me out. You say something and I want to guffaw and slap my knee." He stretched and yawned.

"Sex, blushing, and humor," she added it up. "That's all?"

"I couldn't endure the thought of leaving you . . ."

"Oh, Garret . . ."

". . . and risking your becoming interested in some other man. Of him kissing you, and undoing your buttons, and putting his hands on you." He gave her a quick kiss, then asked, "Why did you marry me?"

She admitted, "I honestly don't know. Except that whenever you left me, I was devastated. I've never cried so much in my entire life, and I wanted only to be with you." She considered him, then said, "Actually we don't know each other very well."

"We'll learn. We can pretend it was an arranged marriage, and we'll spend some of our time getting acquainted."

"Can you imagine my parents arranging my marriage to you?"

"I'm beginning to suspect they put up the barricades just to challenge me. They must know I can't resist a challenge. They probably took one look at me and decided I was it, and how could they best trap me. I think they're smarter than I've given them credit for.

"There I was, innocent, on a mission of grief, vulnerable, and they had this excess daughter they had to find a way to get rid of . . ."

"I beg your pardon!" She started to flounce away.

He held her in bed while she struggled. "Don't struggle! I've just been telling you I can't resist a challenge! You're being deliberately inflaming!"

"I am not!" she shouted.

"See? Opposition! It drives me mad!" He leaned over, rubbing his whiskers into her neck and breathing heavily into her ear.

She squealed and wiggled and writhed, and he loved it. His hands cupped her breasts and he squeezed her tightly against his aroused body. Then he held her down and began to move deeply within her. She excited him by pretending to protest, struggle, thrash, tease, tickle, laugh, shriek, gasp, and grab—and he brought her to paradise once more.

They never did have dinner. They devoured all the hors d'oeuvres, drank the last of the champagne, and straightened up their tumbled bed. Then they curled up together with contented sighs and slept.

CHAPTER THREE

The next morning it was so lovely to lie in bed together that it was after eleven when they finally went to breakfast. As he ate, Garret said they had to get organized and she had to behave, or they'd never get to where they were going.

"You know, I don't know where we're going. Did you give Mother our address?"

"Of course. It's a box number, and I gave her a telephone number where we can be reached." He was paying more attention to the stewed apples.

"A phone number? Won't it be ours?" she asked incredulously.

"It's a direct line to the installation. We have an extension," he said matter-of-factly.

She hesitated. "I know you work for the government. I assume it is ours?"

"Absolutely."

"What do you actually do?"

"I'm a problem-solver. They've given me leave to say that much, but, baby, that's all." He stated it with a firmness that indicated that the topic was not open for discussion.

"If it's that—sensitive—why are they letting me go with you?"

"It wasn't easy," he told her. "But your whole family are good solid citizens."

"You investigated *us?*" she gasped. "That scares me a little."

"No need. It's really routine. It's just that we don't advertise. We're really just a subsidiary radar station."

"No, it's not *just* a radar station," she stated indignantly. "If it were, you'd have said so right away."

"Oh, one of those smarties, huh, just like your parents."

"My . . . parents?"

"Trapped me right into a marriage when I had no intention . . ."

"Garret! Be serious."

"I am! I had no intention of marrying."

"Garret," she said in warning.

"We *are* a subsidiary radar station . . . and just a little more. I'm telling you that because if you observe anything that doesn't fit, we don't want you getting curious or blabbing. Got it? If you feel compelled to speculate about anything you don't understand, do it with me. *No one else.*"

"Yes, sir." She said that smartly, and he laughed.

She was quiet while they packed up the car, but later she sat half-turned in her seat belt, her cheek on the back of her seat, her sleepy eyes on her new husband as she watched how easily he drove. He'd turned his head and smiled at her.

She said, "I can't believe I'm here."

"I never doubted you would be."

She figured he had a short memory. "How could you have been so sure? I wasn't."

"Are you now?" He looked back to catch her lazy smile and again he laughed.

The purr of the motor and the tires' swift passage lulled her. She yawned and her eyes grew heavier and heavier until they closed and she slept.

Garret drove on, and now and again he glanced at his wife, and the feeling of protective, possessive tenderness filled him. He'd won. She was there. She was his.

When they got "there," it was a garage, a motel, and a café out in the middle of nowhere. Tired, they got out and moved around stiffly. Garret was greeted by a man in light-blue cotton coveralls. They talked quietly together, and he nodded to Piper but he didn't offer to speak with her.

The Raymonds went to the café to find their dinners ready and no other diners. They ate in silence and when they'd finished they simply got up and left.

She whispered, "Don't you have to pay?"

"I'm on per diem."

"What's that?"

"Paid travel."

"This is a government place? What if some ordinary person came along and wanted to eat or needed to stay the night or had to have their car fixed?" Her head stayed still but her eyes darted.

"It's done. They'd pay the going rates. There are superb mechanics here."

Then, when they got to the motel, she felt so known, for they'd investigated her. She became tense and asked, as she looked around carefully, "How do we know the place isn't . . . bugged?"

". . . with a movie camera with infrared lights to take naughty pictures?"

"Well . . ." She moved in little huffy motions defensively.

"Trust me."

"I do trust you, but I find our government is tricky," she argued.

"No, they're not. They are very serious, and they're on our side. And the people I work with and under are good people. They wouldn't harm us or embarrass us."

"Just the same . . ."

"Oh, baby, for Pete's sake . . . my God, now I'm saying it." He shook his head. "Come here and kiss me and tell me you're mad for me."

She gave a last look around, then she went to him slowly and wrapped her arms around him and leaned her head against his chest.

His voice rumbled under her ear. "Shall I shave?"

A small smile began and she shook her head.

In a low husky voice he said, "So you like my whiskers?"

"I'm glad you have the right kind. My dad rubs his whiskers into my mother's neck all the time and makes her squeal."

"And you grew up in that kind of depraved atmosphere? Mercy to goodness, a whiskering father and a mother who squeals." And he shook his head and tsked.

She kissed his chin. He made his mouth available. She kissed a corner of it. He adjusted the range. She kissed the other corner. He took her head in his hands and held it so he could kiss her squarely. She sighed against his mouth, and leaned her body softly against his, then moved her arms tighter around him and stroked his back with her hands.

"Where did you learn to do that?" He frowned at her.

"Last night, and here's something else I learned . . ." She deliberately licked her lip, and he groaned and twisted as if that alone tormented him; then she opened her mouth a little as she kissed his and flicked her tongue along his lip.

He prolonged the open-mouthed kiss sweetly, and he touched his tongue to hers. When he released her mouth, he lifted his head back and exhaled. "Whooossssh! Mrs. Raymond, it's just a good thing you're married to me, because you just went past the point of no return."

"Return?" She primly raised inquiring brows. "I've not been anywhere, so how could I 'return?' "

"Baby, you're about to take a trip." He got her zipper caught, and she had to help him. He assured her, "As I practice, I'll get better at it."

"So you've never undressed a woman?"

"Once. A cute little blonde."

Piper stiffened and drew up straight; she stopped undressing and turned flaring eyes to him.

Discarding his shirt, he grinned. "My niece. Two years old. My older sister's kid and a little doll."

"Oh? Did you tell me about her?" She frowned, trying to remember his family at the wedding.

"Somehow I'm not in the mood to talk about my family." He was peeling off his socks.

"What are you in the mood for?" She smiled alluringly at him as he shot a quick glance at her.

"You're just about to find out."

And she did.

* * *

The next day they drove the pickup they had gotten from the garage through worsening desert. It was barren, hot, and very different from Illinois. Everything was strange. It was afternoon when they arrived.

Theirs was the only house. The only obvious house. There was a perfectly normal radar dish and a small building and a shed . . . and their house. The rest of the living quarters and the lab were under a continuous roof that snaked along, faithfully following the contours of a bluff. One need never go out into the sun because there was the long overhang above the walkway that went from living quarters to lab to pool.

Their house was one-story, quite charming, and furnished out of a Sears catalogue. The twin beds had been strapped together with wide webbing, there was champagne in the refrigerator, and the place was spotless.

All of Garret's coworkers were older than he, mostly much older. There were some young guards, but they were out around the area, and she seldom saw them.

She was the only woman. That made a difference, of course, for she had no one with whom to spend her idle time. The men were courteous to her, but they didn't have the need for more than casual conversation with her. They asked her how she was. They said she was so pretty to have around, and they were glad she was there. Then they seemed not to know anything else to say.

After a time she began to feel restless and discontented. She'd never been so alone, and she missed her family. She had thought at first that Garret's being away so much was only a temporary immersion in his work or catching up with a backlog from his holiday. She assumed it wouldn't always be so, that the long hours he was away from her were a fluke.

But when they continued, she complained to Garret; and he said that in the lab the hours seemed to go into some sort of time warp and they got lost. He was sorry.

Occupying her time to her satisfaction became a problem. She'd always done handwork. It was one of the things her mother had taught her that all women should know. But there is a limit to how much lace one can make just to fill time. While Garret viewed and duly admired her completed works, he pretended to worry that she'd add a frill or two to his underwear.

As the months passed, with Garret in the lab such long hours, she became more and more unhappy. If she'd had any training in drawing or painting, that might have saved her, but no one had ever suggested that she paint what was in her mind or how she felt, and it never occurred to her to do that.

She didn't know what materials she needed, and she wasn't confident or bold enough to find out on her own, just to have a go at it and blunder along, learning that way. She did experiment with a child's tray of watercolors, copying the colors of the desert, but the results held no meaning for her, and she lay them in her folder and forgot them. She drew what she knew how to draw, and what she did draw bored her.

Hiking away from the station was assiduously discouraged, so, for exercise, she swam. The rigid rule was never to swim alone. Since everyone else had duties, she had to wait for evening to swim. The men would troop to the pool before supper, some would swim ponderous laps in their special roped-off area, while the others, avoiding her, played boisterously. She swam laps.

The roofed pool was lovely, large, and the sides of the oddly shaped covering were open to the hot desert air. She figured the roofing was to prevent evaporation of the pool's water. She wondered if its molding had anything to do with the wind? To keep it from blowing away?

She'd asked Garret about that, but he'd been distracted by her body and just made a throaty sound. Whether that meant she'd guessed right or only that he was aroused, she didn't know.

It was amazing that she didn't get pregnant. She wondered if she should go to the doctor in the nearest town to see if he could tell her why she hadn't. But, then, she thought, having a baby as the solution to her loneliness wasn't the answer to her problem.

With no hospital and no school, there wasn't even any volunteer work to be done. There was nothing. Piper would scold herself that she should count her blessings. She was healthy, she was married to a man she loved, and she had a nice house. And she had another day.

She asked Garret why he never talked to her. He replied he did talk to her. She said that he greeted her, asked how she was doing, and then she lost him to the mail, the paper, a scratch pad, or to making love. She needed someone to talk to.

He nodded and said, "You probably want an in-depth discussion. I just can't. After the kind of days I have, to come home to an intense conversation about the whys and wherefores and the meaning of life would be like running the Boston marathon then coming home and have you wanting me to go jogging with you. By the time I get home, metaphorically speaking, I'm already limping."

"But I'm desperate for conversation. Why can't you give me some of your time? Why did you marry me, if you don't want to be with me?" Piper pleaded.

"Don't think that I don't want to be with you, Piper.

I do. I married you to keep you in my house, to look at you, to sleep with you." He ignored her sound of impatience. "For you to smile at me, look pretty for me, to be my hostess . . . say, baby, let's have a party this coming Saturday night!" And he beamed, because he'd solved her restlessness.

So they had a party almost every Saturday night. She served a smorgasbord; the men smiled and nodded to her as they talked—together. They all loved coming there. And when they left, they all thanked her for a great evening, and Garret would grin and take her to bed.

But things didn't change and she'd complain, and he'd say, "Pretend I'm a sea captain who manages to sleep in port in spite of the voyage." But some nights he'd sleep at the lab. "Well, you know I can't be fooling around!" he'd laugh. "There's nobody to fool around with!" Then he'd hug her and tell her he hadn't any desire for anyone else. She was all he wanted. And he'd pet her and tease her into smiling for him.

There came a morning that was another of those when Garret had left their bed before she wakened. She'd gone to sleep alone the night before and he hadn't made love to her, so she knew he'd been there only because his pillow was rumpled, most of the covers were on his side and thrown back, and his clothes were on the chair, the floor, and hung on the doorknob of the door to the bathroom.

She lay there wondering why she should get up. She wasn't especially hungry. What was she to do with the day? Another day.

Finally she made herself roll out of bed, and she shivered in the air-conditioning because Garret always turned it up when he came home. She readjusted it, dressed, and made the bed. That took ten minutes. She ate and read yesterday's paper, then watched *Good Morning America.* That there could be a whole other world out there was unreal.

By then it was eight thirty. She picked up Garret's clothes to put in the wash. Going through the pockets, she found a note torn from a scrap of paper: "Tell Mrs. R. there will be someone at the pool so she can swim all day and train for the Olympics. T." So her desperation had been noted, exercise seemed the solution, and the pool was the answer.

That was how Piper became acquainted with Peter Kendricks. He was her age, and he'd joined the army to get some training and experience. Poor Peter Kendricks. There he was at an isolated outpost, bored, young, a self-proclaimed adventurer . . . and he had pulled baby-sitting duty for an equally young, restless, lonely, lovely wife.

That first morning, when she arrived at the pool, Peter had, of course, been expecting her. He watched her walk across the open space from their house, and he'd felt strange. He decided that was just because she was so pretty, and they'd be alone. No one swam during the day.

Having grown up with her male cousins and her two brothers, Piper wasn't even very aware of Peter. She smiled and nodded a courteous hello, put her hat on the chair, unselfconsciously slid out of her robe, and draped it over the back of the chair and stepped out of her sandals. She was totally oblivious of her delectable, shapely silhouette against the already glaring hot sunscape . . . and of Peter's sharply indrawn breath. She went to the edge of the pool, dived cleanly in, and began her long, leisurely strokes.

When eventually Piper finished swimming, she took off

63

her goggles and cap and climbed out at the opposite end of where Peter was sitting, and she leaned over to wrap a towel around her hair. She took up her robe and slung it around her shoulders, stepped into her sandals, and, with a casual wave in his direction, she walked back to her house. She didn't even know his name, nor did she care.

That was about the same routine the next day too, but when she arrived on the third morning, Peter was waiting for her at the point she entered the pool area. He was a good-looking, well-built young man, confident in his brief trunks. Piper glanced at him as she smiled a casual good morning.

"Good morning, Mrs. Raymond." He said it with easy humor.

"Isn't your name Kennerly?"

"Kendricks," he corrected, and then he added, "Peter."

She laughed. "I'm Piper." And together they recited "Peter Piper picked a peck of pickled peppers," and they laughed again.

That set the tone of their relationship—easy, casual, friendly, and it stayed that way . . . for her. He paced her laps to give himself something to do and, when they finished, she went back to the house.

The next day they exchanged a few more remarks during her rest breaks, and after that they both had things saved up to say or to laugh about. Her stroke improved, her laps increased, and Peter was complimentary.

She said it must be marvelous to swim as easily as he did. He replied it came from a lot of idle hours. She could understand idle time. He said he'd learned to play the guitar the same way—too much time. She asked if he played the sax? He said not yet. And he smiled at her.

The day after that he had the guitar with him, and after

they swam for a while he played it for her. He was good at that too.

Having a companion cheered her somewhat. Her life still had no purpose, but her time went more pleasantly. She was getting more exercise, she ate better, felt better, and she had something to look forward to every day.

Piper didn't deliberately set out to seduce Peter. To her he was a long-sought friend. And innocently she firmly believed that men and women could be just good friends. But when she had told Garret how she felt, he had said, if a couple claim that they are just friends, one of them is lying. That in any male-female relationship, one wants sex. Piper protested that he judged everyone by himself, all he ever thought about was sex. He nodded and replied, that was true—around her.

Whenever she asked Garret questions about his beliefs or about hypothetical situations, he would reply, "It's unsolvable until you're actually in that situation" or "How in hell would I know?" or "Why dig that up? It won't change history" or "Talking about that's a waste of time."

But that was the point: She had the time to waste. But Peter would think about her questions, and they'd talk about them and speculate. They found their discussions interesting. He was good-natured, he was humorous, and he listened to her. The days went by.

They met every morning for their swim. They greeted each other with smiling hellos and chatted and visited and swam and talked and laughed. She knew he was there because he'd been ordered there for her sake, and she appreciated that.

She rarely mentioned Garret because Garret had never given any opinions on the subjects she discussed with

Peter. The only things she really had in common with Garret were food and sex. Garret ate anything she put in front of him and said it was great—with no qualifying comments. So when she and Peter talked about food, she had nothing to quote from Garret. She and Peter didn't talk about sex.

Peter thought about it, dreamed of it with her. She went home to Garret and her body was satisfied. Peter struggled with his desire. Even so, at his age, he knew the difference between inadvertent and deliberate enticement. Women his age were either unaware or too blatant, and he knew that Piper didn't "see" him.

He was so excruciatingly aware of her that he began to try to attract her attention to his own body. He'd move things and talk to her while doing it so that her glance was drawn to him. He'd stand above her on the side of the pool and talk to her so that she had to look up at him.

She did notice he had a well-shaped body, from his wide shoulders to his muscular legs. But he still could not compare with the more mature Garret, whose neck and shoulders were a bit heavier, whose stomach was rock-hard, and whose arms and legs were steel muscles wrapped just under the hair-shadowed, tanned flesh.

Since she'd always left the pool area after she'd finished the day's laps, Peter contrived to find reasons for her to stay a little longer, first with talk, then the guitar, and finally Ping-Pong, which she played with delight. She told him how comfortable he was to be around. She supposed it was because they were becoming good friends.

He wasn't comfortable; he was in agony. He longed to touch her. He'd look at her, lying back, eyes closed, hair still sleek with water, her body relaxed against the chair, and he'd ache to hold her, to be that chair. He wanted to touch his lips to her mouth, to peel off that wet suit and to caress her water-cooled body with his hot hands, to cover that soft, rounded form with his own hard, demanding one. And he'd have to shift about and breathe deeply to distract himself.

Once when his desire for her almost overwhelmed him, and his head went back and his face grimaced from the onslaught of emotion, she glanced up at the pause in his music just as his anguished eyes came back down to her.

With a complete lack of understanding she smiled cheerily in sympathy and said, "That sort of music makes me feel that way too. It's almost like a sweet pain. Saxophone music especially affects me that way. I have some great tapes. They're fantastic to dance to. Would you like to hear them?"

Craftily and guilelessly he replied, "I never learned to dance."

She couldn't believe that. Well, they'd just have to remedy that immediately! Would he like to learn?

And, with the bland expression of one for whom the tide is too strong to fight any longer, he said he would, and his voice was only a little shaky.

Everyone at the station had been watching Piper and Peter. And the more animated she became, the closer the men watched Garret. Was he so obtuse to what was happening? Who was going to tell him? What if he knew and was ignoring it? They'd all decided it was really none of their business.

For the first dancing lesson Peter intently watched as Piper demonstrated the basic square, step step step together, step. Then he'd manage the dance with clodhopper grace, his face serious. Her confidence faltered, and she fleetingly wondered if she should wear army boots.

Then as she began to show him how to hold her, he'd slammed her tightly against him—at last. But instead of melting to him, as he'd dreamed, she squirmed and protested he'd just broken three of her ribs! That he was not to treat a partner as if she were going to try to escape. She'd meant that to be funny.

But then he stood too far from her, for her closeness had aroused him, and his face was troubled, his breathing quick, and his hands and body trembled.

Her heart went out to the awkward, tense young man so grimly trying to learn a skill and so vulnerable to failure. That's really what she thought. And, of course, in her innocence her judgments were wrong.

Very kindly, she instructed him. She complimented him when she could find something that he did right. He was stiff and wooden; he crowded against her, tripped her, caught her. He held her close, but he never once stepped on her feet. That should have clued her in, but she was so earnestly trying to help him to succeed, it never occurred to her that only a skilled dancer could be so beautifully clumsy.

It was later that week that she first took their lunch to the pool. He was delighted and praised the food and her cooking skills and made appreciative sounds as he ate, licking his lips and sighing in contentment.

She said she bet his mother was glad when he went into the army and she didn't have to pay for his groceries anymore. He said Piper was almost as good a cook as his mother. She scoffed, saying she didn't believe that for a minute, but that he was so hungry all the time that anything tasted good. He denied that, saying he was sure she'd had special training. Yes, she said, her mother.

"That's all? No French chefs standing around twirling their moustaches, instructing you and pinching you?"

"Not a one."

"Aw," he said, "too bad. I don't have a moustache, but I can pinch." He looked elaborately lecherous.

"You're too young for a moustache." She studied him judiciously. "But I'll bet Garret would look smashing in one."

He didn't want to discuss Garret, so he rolled to his feet, tugged Piper to hers, and said there was enough time to play Ping-Pong and to settle their stomachs before they swam an additional number of laps to compensate for that superior chocolate cake.

That night, just as she was getting into bed, Garret came in. He asked her to come sit with him while he had a piece of the chocolate cake. So, pulling on a loose short-sleeved floor-length wrapper, she went into the kitchen and sat sleepily on a stool with her bare feet tucked up on a rung.

As he cheerfully cut a large slice from what was left of the cake, he commented, "Listen, baby, if you're going to gobble that much cake, you'll get fat."

"Oh, it wasn't me so much." She yawned. "It was Peter. He loves chocolate cake."

"Peter?" Garret tried to place the name.

"Kendricks. My baby-sitter."

"Oh, yes. He's just about your age, as I recall. He'd better watch the chocolate, he'll get zits."

She ignored that and asked, "Have you ever had a moustache?"

"Oh, sure. We all go through that stage. It's a little like girls getting Orphan Annie frizzes at least once."

"Would you notice me if I frizzed my hair?" She yawned again.

"I'd notice you if you were bald." He put his glass, fork, and plate into the sink, then he went to her and put his hands out to lift her from the stool, but he pretended he couldn't locate her armpits and therefore had to hunt for them around her loosely covered body. She became less sleepy. He suggested, "Let's go listen to your saxophone tapes and get you in the mood."

"In what mood?" She smiled and her eyes looked at him flirtatiously.

"I'm planning on tumbling you," he informed her in an off-handed way.

"Oh? Tumbling . . . is that part of the Army's physical fitness program: calisthenics and gymnastics?"

He nodded profoundly. "I've carried the exercise a step further."

"Do they know?"

"Not yet. I haven't perfected it." He sighed a burdened sigh of a man with many cares. "It still needs lots of practice—to refine the movements."

"I see. How fine they have such a dedicated man in you."

He cast a wicked look at her. "I'd rather be the dedicated man in . . ."

"Why, sir! How can you be so bold?"

"I see I must explain how much the country's health depends on your cooperation in this vital research." By then he'd eased her down on the sofa and began to look for the tapes. She lay back, watching him with a slight smile, very relaxed. He asked, "Where are the tapes? I thought they were right here."

She roused, sat up, then remembered, "Oh, I must have left them over at the pool."

"At the pool? You swim to them?"

"Oh, no." She smiled. "I'm teaching Peter to dance."

"To *those* tapes? What are you trying to do? Seduce the poor kid? You know I can't allow that." But he wasn't serious. Only as an afterthought, he asked, "How long are you over there each day?"

"Just about the whole day. We swim, and dance, and play Ping-Pong . . ."

"Ping-Pong? When you get really good, tell me, and I'll beat you." He dropped down next to her on the sofa and curled his arms around her willing body, pulling her close to him.

"You can try."

"Think you're pretty good, huh." His amusement was reflected in his deep voice, and he leaned his face into her neck, delicately rubbing it with his budding whiskers.

"I can beat Peter with my paddle hand tied behind my back." She was very smug as she moved her neck closer to him.

"He must be deliberately letting you win." He opened the buttons of her wrapper.

She became indignant. "Now, why would you say a thing like that?"

"Indignation arouses me." His voice was hoarse and his breath hot.

"I think it was the chocolate cake."

"The cake?" He wasn't really interested.

"You were already propositioning me in the kitchen."

"Oh, that. It was because you yawned. Yawning gets to me."

"Everything does."

His voice husky, he said, "Just you." His mouth moved up her jaw, across her cheek, and nibbled her lips. As she sighed and turned so that she could be even closer, he suggested, "Why don't you undress me, and I'll lie here, and you can take unfair advantage of me? I'll try not to squeal or struggle or cry out."

And he was very brave and didn't, although he did moan and gasp a little.

In the next month Peter's progress in dancing was amazing. He could easily do the box step, move into the turn, and back her straight across the tiled floor. It was marvelous. His right hand worked just perfectly in guiding her and holding her steady, and she was enormously pleased. His conscience only twinged as she bragged, "I'm not even aware you're counting."

But as the days went by she began to worry about him. He wasn't as lighthearted as he had been. "Are you worried about something?" she asked, frowning with concern.

"No," he replied, but his eyes were serious, and she had to work to make him smile.

"Are you feeling all right?" she questioned him at other times. He wasn't eating with his usual appetite.

"Just fine. No problem." He hesitated, then asked very seriously, "Have you ever had an affair since you've been married?"

"Oh, no." She was amused.

"I seriously doubt if your . . . if Garret would mind. He's modern enough, and everyone does it these days."

"Not me," she disagreed firmly.

"Don't be narrow-minded. All you have of life are your experiences, and you should have an affair to round out your life."

"And rob a bank?" She laughed at the silliness.

"Don't be childish!" he commanded and his voice was harsh.

She stared at him, then frowned. This wasn't her carefree companion.

That night, in bed, after Garret had pointedly turned over so that his back was to her as he tried to sleep, Piper couldn't shut up. She talked about a letter she'd had from Jennifer that dissected the manners and mores of the rest of the family, and a printed card with ghoulish drawings from Robert, then, after Garret had grunted a couple of times in reply to questions, she asked, "Would you mind terribly if I had an affair?"

"Yes!" His tone clearly indicated that was the end of the conversation.

"Oh." She seemed surprised. "Peter said you wouldn't care, that you're civilized and, anyway, everyone does it."

He didn't reply and the silence lengthened. Piper turned over, stretched her well-toned muscles, yawned, and went peacefully to sleep.

But on the other side of the bed Garret was definitely wide awake. He lay for a long time, frowning into the darkened room, and thinking. As if in replay, he heard in his brain the comments Piper had been making the last few months to his half-listening ears: "Peter swims very well. Peter says . . . He thinks . . . Peter likes . . . Peter doesn't . . . . . . teaching Peter . . . Peter. Peter. Peter." Good God, what was going on around there?

The next morning at breakfast Garret sat watching Piper. She hummed around the cheery little room. Garret wondered what that meant. Was she anticipating seeing Kendricks? Were they already having an affair? If she were having an affair, did that affect his feeling for her?

No. She was his. Why would she want a kid like Kendricks? It would have to stop. He asked his wife, "What time do you go over to the pool?"

"About nine."

"You eat lunch there?"

"Umm-hmm. Today we're having ham salad." Then she added carelessly, "Want to join us?"

Did she mean that, or was she trying to throw him off the track? Watching her face as she stirred the scrambled eggs, he asked, "What do you do with him?" Make love? Tease? Kiss under the water with your hands groping and touching?

"Oh, we just talk. He has a good sense of humor, and he's willing to talk about anything."

Yeah, like having affairs with my wife and being sure I'm "civilized" enough not to care? He's rattled the wrong cage. Aloud he said, "I may be free at noon. You might add a sandwich for me—if it's not too much trouble." He added that last with calculation.

"Would you really?"

But he qualified it. "I'll have to see." His good-bye kiss was long and possessive.

It was almost eleven when Garret walked into the pool area wearing swim trunks. Piper was in the water, clinging to the side of the pool while Peter stood above her showing off his body in what Garret thought was a blatant manner. Peter caught Garret's movement from the corner of his eye and turned, alert to the threat.

When Peter's eyes swung away from her, Piper turned curiously to see what had attracted his attention—and there was Garret! "Garret!" she yelled in exuberant delight, and shoved away from the side of the pool to swim toward him. Both men knew her preference; it couldn't be faked.

Peter stood there watching as Piper tore across the pool, effortlessly pulled herself from the water, and reached for Garret. But he put his hands on her shoulders, fending her off, and, laughing, he complained, "You're wet and cold! Get away from me, woman." And his very words showed his smug confidence in her love.

"You came early!" she said excitedly. "You're here!"

"Did you fix me a sandwich?" he demanded in mock belligerence.

"I fixed you two! Oh, Garret, I'm so glad you're here." Piper ran her fingers into her dripping hair and shook the droplets at Garret, who protested and lunged for her, but she turned and dived back into the water. He followed, and they chased and played. He caught her and rolled her over, clasped her intimately to him and, just before he submerged them, he sent one more look at Peter.

When they surfaced, her face was pink from his attentions and he grinned at her, quite satisfied. She wound her arms around his neck and allowed him to keep them afloat, and she clung and giggled and squealed—and neither of them saw Peter's silent departure.

It wasn't until lunchtime that Piper realized that Peter was gone. She'd shrugged with a grin. "I suppose he figured you could baby-sit me." And if nothing had convinced him, that did.

He left her in bed the next morning, and when she arrived at the pool, it was Garret who waited for her. She was so genuinely, happily surprised that he only then began to appreciate the scope of her feelings for him. They swam, enjoyed each other's company, but when they'd finished the laps for that session, he went back to the lab and she was alone.

It was several days before she found out that Peter had been transferred. She'd inquired on the fifth day, concerned that he might be ill. She told Garret, "I'm not surprised he's left."

"Oh?" he questioned cautiously.

"He really wasn't happy here. He'd become gloomy, and he wasn't eating well. I believe he was lonely for other people his age." She wasn't aware she was stating her own case. "But he didn't say good-bye. I think that's strange. I know he was only there so I could swim, but I'd really thought of him as a friend who'd helped me pass the time."

"He was in love with you." He told her that, but he didn't give her Peter's note.

"Don't be silly."

"He was," Garret insisted.

"Good God, Garret, just because you find me attractive, doesn't mean every other man is lusting after me."

"He was learning to play the sax," he told her, as if that was proof enough.

"You mean every saxophone player has learned to play the sax because I like saxophones?" she hooted.

Fortunately he let it go at that.

For almost a month, Garret was there every morning at ten, and she came to expect him. She relished the time. He appeared to. But there did come the day when he wasn't there. She waited and was turning away to go back to the house when one of the older men came hurrying out carrying a sheaf of papers, apologizing for being late. He sat down in the lounge and sorted things out and ignored her.

After that all the older lab men took turns. They read manuals, sorted papers, wrote furiously, talked on the phone in gruff tones and gestures. And she knew she was a nuisance. That went on for another month.

The next Saturday night, she made the announcement she was no longer going to swim in the daytime. They were released from the responsibility. There were such cries of sincere protest and they became so agitated that there was nothing for her to do but continue to swim.

She began to explain to Garret that she needed more from her life. But her talking to him was something similar to her talk about Peter and her words didn't penetrate. Or Garret didn't want to hear.

They went on leave, but when they returned the days continued as before. She would lie in bed wondering what difference anything made and whether she should get up or stay in bed. That was the beginning of dangerous thinking.

Then her struggle to survive caused her to react in unusual ways, and she became defiant. As with anything that is confined, she felt driven by the need to know the limits of her prison, so she walked out, exploring the desert. She felt a kinship with the wasteland; its life was as sparse and bleak as hers.

Garret told the others to allow her wanderings, that she was restless and the exercise was good for her. He said for them to leave her alone.

She did wear her hat and she walked in the early hours or those of the late afternoon. She wore the correct clothes and carried a water flask. She wore a sunscreen and sensi-

77

ble, leather, snakeproof, calf-high boots. She carried a stout stick and a whistle. If she got lost, a whistle would come in handy.

And eventually she did get lost. By accident one of the guards came across her stumbling in the desert and instantly knew she didn't have her canteen or stick. He hurried to her, approached her slowly, and spoke, "Hello, Mrs. Raymond, got yourself lost?"

She replied through cracked lips, "Not at all."

The guard's eyes flared. She was worse off than he'd suspected. He said, "Let me help you over this rough spot." Then, as he led her, he very cleverly pressed a nerve, and she slid into unconsciousness. He poured his full reserve supply of water gently over her head and wet her lips as he spoke into the wafer-radio to tell them to send a chopper.

It was almost two weeks before she recovered. "I saw a snake," she'd told several of them at different times, seeming completely lucid. "He was as dusty as the stones, and he smiled at me. He said, 'Go back,' but I knew he was an illusion. There was that snake in the Garden, you remember." And they'd nod and hold her hand and worry.

She didn't know Garret. When he sat by her bed she would tell him also, "You must tell Garret Raymond I am all right. G-a-r-r-e-t R-a-y-m-o-n-d." She spelled it slowly, as if it were difficult for her to sort it out. "If he's busy, leave a note for him."

That a note would have to be left telling him his wife was alive almost killed him. "Oh, baby," he groaned. "I'm here beside you. You're all right. You're home." His voice was rough and husky with emotion.

78

"I'm home?" She was puzzled. "Where's Mama?" And she'd look beyond him and fret.

A cold finger touched Garret's heart. Home to her meant her mother? Not him? The unwanted worry edged in as to why she'd wandered so far. Where had she been going? Leaving? What was he doing to her? But he shoved the thoughts away and turned resolutely from them. She was going to be all right. She was there—with him.

CHAPTER FOUR

The days passed and even though it was winter, she still wasn't allowed in the sun at all. As her strength returned, she began to swim again, and her revolving order of sitters beamed at her and nodded. Gradually the same old routine had returned—except that she was forbidden to go into the desert and her cage was infinitely smaller.

She again read all the current events magazines and watched all the PBS programs, but she had no one to discuss them with. She chose a professional basketball team to root for and learned their names and the points they'd scored. She judiciously watched the spring-training films of the baseball teams but faced the fact that baseball wasn't very exciting. She made her own TV dinners and ate them while she watched the evening news. And she played solitaire.

The Saturday-night buffets continued. She furnished the food and accepted the compliments—and she finally faced the fact that she was going to leave Garret. She had come to this decision over the past few weeks and now she was determined to do it.

One night she finally told him, and he scoffed. She got mad and quarreled with him. He was tender and carried her around and sat in the big wooden rocker and cradled her. He babied her and she cried. He assumed it was time for her period.

She explained carefully just exactly how she felt, and he was irritated. She wondered that with all the problem-solvers at that lab why couldn't someone solve her problem? And he thought he did: He made love to her. But for Piper it wasn't enough. She resolved that morning she would leave.

Lonely days later Piper's living room was filled with the sounds and movements of the large man who enthusiastically praised her husband's achievement in solving a problem in the lab that had had all of them stumped for months.

"Your husband is phenomenal! The dedication of that man is awesome. No one else came even close. You know, he's been at it night and day for . . ."

"I know, Tom." Piper stood watching him with calm blue eyes. She wore a blue-and-white striped seersucker suit, and there was no blouse under the buttoned, short-sleeved jacket. Her sandals were thin lines of leather. Her dark hair was twisted neatly and secured on top of her head, and large sunglasses had been pushed up past her forehead. It was obvious she'd been ready to leave the house.

Although Tom had automatically closed the door against the heat to save the air-conditioning, she hadn't asked the big, arm-waving man to sit down. She regarded him with patience.

"Garret should be here any minute. This was a real breakthrough." Tom shook his head contritely. "I'm just sorry *he* didn't get to tell you."

Her smile was kind as she reassured him, "That's okay."

He moved then to pace restlessly. "I was so excited when I heard he'd done it, but he wasn't at the lab, and I just had to see him. He's been working at it almost nine months!"

"Yes," she agreed. "About the time it takes to have a baby." Now, why had she said that?

He stopped pacing, and his eyes fell involuntarily to her flat stomach. "Oh? Are you . . . ?" There was the beginning of a smile.

"No, Tom."

The conversation was canceled by a vehicle's powerful rush to a halt, the sound of a roughly closed door; then firm, hurried strides came toward the house.

Tom turned a grin to Piper as he needlessly announced, "It's Garret!" He swung the door open just as Garret reached for it, and Garret's brief surprise was overwhelmed by Tom's congratulations, which included hearty shoulder thumps and a wringing handclasp. But Garret's gray eyes had gone past Tom's shoulder to smile at Piper and, as he winked, his glance flicked down over her as he noted what she wore.

Three or four times Tom said, "Well, I'll be going now . . ." before he could actually tear himself away. When the door was finally closed after him, the silence was marked.

"Congratulations." Piper smiled at her husband.

His eyes examined her. "Where are you going?"

Her smile faded. "Home," she replied as her chin lifted.

His body jerked in brief exasperation. "That again!" He jabbed a finger toward the floor. "*This* is your home. You're in it!" He strode to the windows and snapped the drapes closed to dim the room against the constant glare of the desert sun.

To avoid arguing she said, "I'm glad you were successful." Then she glanced at her watch and added, "Are you hungry? I have time to fix you something."

"Breakfast . . ."

She raised inquiring brows. "At this time of the afternoon? Haven't you eaten?"

"Breakfast . . . tomorrow." He turned back to her.

"That was charmingly said," she commended him.

"I wasn't being charming." He took her glasses carefully from her hair, and she didn't resist. "You're staying here with me." He gathered her close against him.

Her hands slid around his waist and clasped behind his back. She tilted her head up until their eyes locked, then she gently shook her head, denying she would stay.

Tightening his arms, he pressed her body closer to his. He deliberately moved his face on hers, then his mouth explored the familiar taste of her skin as he breathed under her ear, and his hands moved knowingly along her back.

"Ahhhh," she sighed in sad appreciation. "You are an expert. I hope your next wife is a fertile, contented homemaker, a home ec major who loves bridge and knitting and housekeeping . . ." She paused poignantly. "And waiting."

His rough voice protested in a teasing way. "I don't want a paragon. I want you." He slowly moved his mouth along her face and throat as he pressed and released her body in order to feel the roundness of her breasts against his hard chest.

"I wish there were a middle ground, but there just isn't one."

When the phone rang, Garret absently reached to

83

switch off the sound as he replied, "There are all kinds of things to keep you busy . . ."

"I swim two miles a day—doing it in laps." She began the list that had been repeated too many times.

Keeping to his light teasing, he leaned back to glance down at her body. "That's doing great."

In desperation she flung out a hand and objected, "That's total boredom. It's like running two miles on a treadmill . . . if you could endure running in this place. Maybe I could do it in the air-controlled lab—with the other squirrels."

"There aren't any squirrels."

She continued the list. "There's television, sewing, reading . . . I'm forbidden to walk in the desert anymore, and I'm not allowed to go out in the sun."

"I'm partial to pale skin." He slowly unbuttoned her jacket, moving his hands against her breasts, nudging them intimately, then sliding the jacket open to push his hands up under the sides of those bare mounds, lifting their softness with his wrists and bringing her close to him again.

She frowned. "Garret, you're really not listening."

"Yes, I am. I'm listening to my hands on you and the whispering sound as they move on your skin. You are so smooth and lovely."

"Garret . . ." She tried to continue her protest, but the sensations curling through her body began to distract her.

He released the clasps that held her hair to allow the silken mass to fall free as he turned her face up to his, and he kissed her. It was long and very skillful. As their mouths parted, he said huskily, "Listen to that. That soft sound of our lips touching, which is the second most exciting sound in this world. The most exciting is when

our bodies meet. Ahhh. The way you smell thrills me."
His hands moved in pleasure, molding her closer, and his
body curved to hers as it tensed.

Still protesting, she said, "Garret . . ." But she was
clinging to him as the flame of desire licked up through
her body and her mouth was eager for him. She forgot
what she'd started so earnestly to say because she was
unbuttoning his shirt. She opened it to press her breasts
against his chest to slowly rub them there, to gasp at the
sensual excitement that flooded her as her tender skin
reacted to the texture of his.

Again he briefly leaned back to see her face, to grin
smugly down at her; his eyes smoldered and the timbre of
his voice roughened as he coaxed, "Make love with me."

Her breathing erratic, she swallowed and blinked to
focus, noting his quick breath, how hot his hands were on
her, and how hard he felt against her softness. "Well
. . ." She raised her widely dilated pupils to his. "I suppose
we could have one for the road." She meant it would be
a final salute to their love.

He thought she was being flippant and laughed. He put
an arm under her knees and lifted her. Then he stood still
to look down at her curled in his arms, her face serious,
her dark hair swinging free. With the toe of the opposite
foot she slid her sandals off, and they dropped to the floor.
He carried her into their bedroom and put one knee on
their bed to lay her carefully in the middle of it.

As he straightened, their eyes met, and she thought,
One more time. I can have him one more time. Then she
allowed her eyes the pleasure of going over him as he
discarded his clothes with careless speed, and her secret
places shivered for him and tingled with her desire. He
was so beautiful. So male. So loved.

85

He slowly eased away the rest of her clothes and tossed them aside. As his fingers flipped her panties back over his shoulder, he stopped motionless to feast his eyes on her loveliness. His mouth parted as his starkly intense face and dark eyes shone with his need for her.

With the room shuttered against the sun's constant glare, she lay in the midst of the sheets, thrilling to his masculinity and to his power as he cherished her precious femininity with his eyes.

He lay carefully beside her, at first protecting her from his weight as his trembling hands lifted and moved her so that he could touch her eagerly. His leg slid up over hers and his hair-rough skin excited the smoothness of hers, and little skitters of excitement quivered over the surface of her skin and sank to deeper places to trigger sensations there.

He teased and stroked her neck with gentle kisses, arousing her nipples to sensitized peaks, driving her into a frenzied awareness of him. And as she clutched at him and gasped, his smile was confident and knowing.

Then her own hands and mouth turned feverish, roaming across his broad chest, her tongue finding the flat nipples and tantalizing them into firm crests. Her hands grazed his hips, then stroked his firm thighs until his eyes became hot gleams of fiery pleasure. She slid up his body to his scalding mouth and pressed herself against his dampened body.

"Do you want me?" he demanded as his low husky voice caught from his labored breathing against her throat.

She clutched him closer, and the deep chuckle in his chest was triumphant.

He maneuvered them and took her with deliciously

exquisite teasing and they moved in luscious torment as their passion burned higher and her body flamed from his touch. His mouth consumed hers, then slid to her ears and the side of her throat.

Nothing that voracious could be sustained and their lovemaking intensified to tumultuous writhings as their breaths became fast and ragged and their hands almost frantic . . . and they shuddered into a world of sensual delight that slowly lessened into sweet memory.

When, at last, they lay satisfied and their breathing and heartbeats were calm again, Garret scoffed indulgently, "And you wanted to leave."

She didn't reply but shifted to move away from him. He stopped her and said sharply, "You're staying." When she didn't speak, he patted her bare bottom and, continuing in his attempt to smooth over the rift with light humor, he teased her. "You got what you wanted. I'll be more assiduous in applying the treatment in the future."

She sighed with the tiredness that comes from repeating old arguments. "Making love isn't everything."

"You like it."

"I love it—with you."

"Then . . . *why?*"

Almost desperate, she said, "Oh, Garret, it isn't the only thing in life."

"It's a good part." He kissed her very sweetly, his voice rough with emotion. "And you're good and I like your parts."

She repeated in a kind of despair, "There's more to life."

Angrily falling back on the bed and biting off the words, he snapped, "I know! You're unfulfilled. A woman's libber. Damn them all! Why can't you be like other women?"

Reasonably she asked in turn, "Why can't you be like other men? Work nine to five and be home?"

His tone turned harsh, "It's my job. You knew it when you married me."

"We go through this same thing every time. I didn't know what your work would be like. You forget that you courted me with every waking minute. How did I know you were going to shut me up in this"—she gestured helplessly—"nothing place, and leave me alone all day and most of the nights? You come home occasionally to make love to me and go right to sleep. We never talk."

Impatiently he growled, "My work's secret, you know that."

"But there are other things we could talk about."

"Other women get along all right."

"Or seem to."

He paused, then suggested in a softer voice, "We could have a kid."

"You know we can't," she responded impatiently. "I've seen more doctors in the past year than I can count, and they still don't know why we can't have a baby."

"We could see about adopting one," he countered.

"Just to occupy my time? That's a poor reason to want a child. You wouldn't be around any more often than you are now. And if I'm going to raise a child alone, why stay here in this desolate, hot, windswept desert?" She had not known two years ago, as she knew now, that their marriage wasn't everything she needed or wanted and that a baby would not change that fact.

He moved restlessly. "We can't live our lives in each other's pockets. We are separate people, Piper. Why can't you find something that interests you? Can't you take some courses or something?" He was trying to turn her away from things they'd argued over too many fruitless times.

"I'm twenty years old, married two years ago right out of high school, and I'm not trained for anything but going on to college. But you came along and dazzled my mind . . ."

". . . and more." He grinned and ran his hands delicately over her naked body.

". . . into becoming a respectably married plaything, waiting patiently at home, exclusively for your attentions —when you remember me."

He rose to lean over her and slowly nuzzled his face against the side of her throat. "You have all my attentions and intentions . . ."

"There you go again!" Impatiently she pushed his head away, holding it so that she could frown into his eyes. "Be serious, Garret! All of our brief encounters are involved in sex."

He grinned and moved his hands on her, turning his head to kiss the wrists of the restraining hands that held his head from her. "Who's knocking it?" And he chuckled in real humor.

But she was cross. "Any woman would do for you. I was gone for two weeks last month and you didn't even notice."

"No, you weren't." He dismissed the thought.

"I was gone for two weeks the end of last month."

"No. You were right here. I may have been up and gone before you got up, and I may have come back home when you were already in bed, but I did sleep here. I made love with you. I may have missed a night or two here or there, but I'm never gone for two weeks." That finished that.

She repeated, "Two weeks at the end of last month."

"Come off it, Piper, I made love to you! You were here."

She denied it, "It wasn't me."

That exasperated him. "*Now* what nonsense are you trying?"

"It was a blonde." She'd worn a blond wig for the two weeks as a test and he hadn't even mentioned it.

"You're being silly, do you realize that?"

Slowly she shook her head. "No."

"It was you." He effortlessly pushed his head forward in spite of her restraining hands and he kissed her. "And you enjoyed every minute"—his tongue licked along her lower lip—"of every time." And he kissed her lovingly.

When he raised his mouth she said, "The blonde undoubtedly did. Anyone would. You're a remarkable lover. But it wasn't me."

He fumed with the beginnings of anger, "You know damned well that you couldn't pull something like that on me. I know you."

"Did you speak to her?"

"*Her?* What in hell do you mean?"

"The blonde who was in your bed for two weeks. Did you talk to her? If you didn't hear her speak, how could you know who it was? Her voice is quite different." She'd practiced it.

He raised himself to sit up on the bed. His body was marvelous in the dim light that filtered through the shuttered windows. She watched the muscles roll under the tanned skin that covered the hard beautiful steel core. He was a powerful, superb male.

He looked down at her, his blond hair rumpled and untidy from their lovemaking. His gray eyes were hidden by the thick dark lashes as his narrowed stare riveted on her. "I don't know what you're trying to prove, unless it's that I don't chitchat." His tone hit the word with derision. "I admit it. But, Piper, don't try to tell me there was another woman in our bed, because there hasn't been. I know you. My hands and body and mouth know you, and no other woman could be like you."

She repeated stubbornly, "She was blond. She used my soap and perfume."

"I may throttle you."

"You don't need me. Any woman would do."

"Would you really put another woman in our bed as some stupid kind of test?" He eyed her angrily. "Could you? I don't believe you are so detached from me emotionally that you could stand to do that."

She sighed and moved to the side of the bed to get up. His troubled glare followed her. Not looking back at him, she went into the bathroom to shower. He was still lying on the bed when she returned and opened her suitcase to take out fresh clothes. She dressed silently, then hung up the suit that he had flung aside.

They didn't speak as she brushed her hair and twisted it on top of her head. Holding it there, she then had to hunt for another clasp, again in her suitcase. When she glanced at her watch, he ground out harshly, "You're not going anywhere."

Quietly she agreed, "It's too late today, but nothing is solved. I'll leave in the morning." When he didn't reply she left the bedroom, calling back, "There are steaks in the refrigerator."

Thoughtfully he lay there for a minute, then he rolled out of the bed and, naked, he followed her into the kitchen and stood watching her. How could she speak so easily of leaving him after they'd made such beautiful love?

Somberly he studied her as she moved about, then

something beyond her caught his glance, and he moved his head to look past her into the dining room. He saw a prettily set table and went to the door to note the flowers and champagne. With a slight frown he turned back to Piper. "A celebration." It was almost a question.

"Yes." Her faint smile was odd. Rueful?

"Boy, you were quick to get the bouquet here. I thought Tom told . . ." His frown deepened, then his face cleared. "Our anniversary!" he exclaimed with regretful laughter. "It was yesterday! My God, no wonder! So hell really hath no fury . . . Now I understand." He went to her and reached for her. "Oh, baby."

But she opened the refrigerator door and took ice from the freezer. "It wasn't that." She moved past him to put the ice around the bottle of champagne and spun it so it would cool.

In a disbelieving humor he exclaimed, "Oh, no." He felt he'd found the real reason for her discontent. His grin broadened. It was all just a female snit for being ignored at the wrong time.

But as she returned to the kitchen she cautioned him, "You have deliberately leaped to the wrong conclusion."

"Don't kid me. You meant to leave and have me find that table all dressed up to celebrate, and you meant to rub my nose in it."

"It was to underline the problem," she corrected him. Then she suggested, "Go get dressed. We might have a chance to talk about it later. Tonight will be the last chance we have to understand each other."

Disregarding that ominous-sounding statement, Garret began to placate her. "I'm sorry I couldn't be here last night, baby, but I do have a present for you."

She smiled faintly and repeated, "Go get dressed."

He teased. "Don't you like me naked?"

With an off-hand, raking glance, she replied, "You're gorgeous."

"See?" He was complacent. "You're not going to leave me."

"Tomorrow morning."

"No." He put his hands on his bare hips, waiting for her to say something so he could argue it all out, but she only cut up the onions and tomatoes into the salad. Finally he turned and left the kitchen.

Not wanting his colleagues to intrude into their private time, Garret lettered a Please Do Not Disturb sign and taped it to their front door. If Piper and Garret had listened, they would have heard the noisy men still celebrating Garret's triumph in the lab. Some of them had trooped to their door, read the sign, and left—laughing.

Piper's anniversary gift to him was a leather-bound address book. Black. A bachelor's little black book? He made no comment as he tossed it aside. She realized he thought she was being nasty, so she explained, "I copied in the addresses from my book that I thought you'd want too."

With that his eyes became more troubled, for her leaving wasn't as impulsive as he'd assumed. He went into their bedroom to fetch her gift and opened his top drawer. There he found his grandmother's ring, which Piper had had as an engagement ring, and with it was a note saying she'd loved wearing something so beautiful, and she thanked him for its loan. A cold feeling touched his heart. This was a mood he could not tease her out of.

Sobered, he returned to the dining room and handed her the ring box. She hesitated before she took it and opened it. It was a lovely blue sapphire. He reached for it and put it on her finger and, watching her, he lifted her hand and kissed the ring.

Her voice was a little unsteady as she said she would treasure it and remember him always.

Piper didn't broach the subject of her departure for the rest of the meal, and Garret had no inclination to bring it up. They finished the miniature pies of crushed strawberries with whipped cream, then they took demitasse cups of coffee to the living room and Garret chose saxophone and piano tapes from their collection. Of course that was deliberate, for the tapes had been a part of their early days, and now, quietly played, they filled Piper with a sad nostalgia, as he had hoped.

He tugged her from her solitary chair and settled her beside him on the sofa. He kissed her sweetly and said with a confidence he didn't necessarily feel, "You'll never leave me."

She drew a shaky breath. "You are a dear man . . . when you're here." She reached up to push his hair back from his forehead, adding, "For once, please, listen. You've known for a long time that I'm unhappy here. There is a limit to the ways I can fill my time alone. The men here are nice and I like them, but they are as busy as you . . ." She trailed off plaintively.

"One of the reasons I was glad you were so young, when I found you, is that I thought you wouldn't be infected by the need to lead a quote—meaningful—unquote life," Garret answered.

She chided his saying that. "There are a great many women who are leading meaningful lives in their homes with and without children. You misunderstand what being a fulfilled woman means.

"If you were a lady raising three kids all by herself and were finally being paid equally to a man doing the same job, you wouldn't think you were leading a meaningless existence."

"The Equal Rights Amendment hasn't been passed yet."

"It's the agitation for it that's called attention to some of the inequalities women have had to put up with."

"It isn't needed."

"Spoken like a man. You know, Garret, if I were a man, I believe I would dislike it as much as you. It would be lovely, I suppose, to have someone you like as a total slave."

"Is that how you feel? That you're a slave?" He was offended.

"I devote my entire time to seeing to your comfort and satisfaction."

He turned his hand out and replied with exasperation, "It couldn't take too much time, if you find it boring."

"If you were here more, I probably wouldn't be bored."

"So it's my fault." He didn't believe it.

"Only partly . . ."

"Thanks a lot."

"Your 'fault' is that I wasn't acquainted with the terms of our marriage. I was too young to understand what being married to a man like you meant. I thought it would go on the way it was when we courted, that I would see you and be with you most of the time."

"I have to support us." He pointed out the obvious as he looked her way.

"No. That isn't it. You have chosen to make a living

95

doing something that interests you so much it occupies most of your time and thoughts."

"What's so wrong in that? Why shouldn't I do what interests me?"

"And why shouldn't I?" she asked in a reasonable way.

He grated, "Women are made to be wives and homemakers."

"Therefore all men are made to be husbands? How about all women are wives and homemakers and all men husbands and farmers? Then it's basic: The women cook the food the men grow it. Could you be a farmer?"

"God, no. I'd never fit the mold."

"Then why expect me to? What if I insisted you farm. Would you?"

He didn't reply for a minute. They were so intent on what they were saying that the saxophone music was wasted on them. Then he told her, "Before we were married you said you wanted children and to live in my house with me."

"There. You have it—to live in your house *with you.*"

"What about children?"

"I didn't marry you to have children. I married you to live with you and be your love—and to have your children. But you're so seldom here."

"It has always been that way," he instructed with marked patience. "All through time the women have stayed home and minded the place, and the men have gone off to sea, or war, or jobs. You should have known how it would be."

"I had no idea. I'm restless and lonely and there has to be more to life than this. Do you realize that in the two years we've lived here I never been inside the lab? I don't even know what you do in there." He shifted his body, ignoring her outburst and looking at her face with calculation. "What it comes down to is that you don't love me."

She replied sadly, "Unfortunately I do."

He leaned away from her, putting his arm along the back of the sofa, sprawling beside her, but available if she wanted to be closer to him. "If you love me, then how could you possibly leave me?"

"I'm not leaving *you*—"

"Good," he interrupted, trying to put an end to the disturbing argument.

But she continued. "I'm leaving a situation. I can't see you changing. You love your work. I'm not as important to you . . ."

He warned, "Piper!"

"No," she earnestly explained. "I understand it. But with our lives as they are, this just isn't enough for me. I want to feel—"

"Fulfilled!"

She chose the word with care. "How about *useful?*"

"You're useful here."

"To you. But that's because your laundry's done, your meals ready whether you show up or not, your house is tidy, and I'm in your bed if you choose to come. But anyone would do."

"I'm getting damned sick and tired of you throwing that in: Anyone would do. I love you, Piper, and you know it. But trying to reason with you is totally hopeless."

She repeated it immediately. "Trying to reason with you is totally hopeless."

By then they were sitting apart, and they stared at each other, hostile and silent.

"You're not leaving here." He was positive.

"How can you prevent it?"

"You're my wife, and I'm bigger than you are." Having reminded them both of that, he almost smiled.

"Physically you can stop me, but you can't imprison me. I will leave. It may take several days, but the lab will find some fascinating problem that no one else can solve, and you'll be gone."

"The work is important." It was a statement of fact.

"I agree. I'm glad they have you. I can't and won't ask you to give it up. Just, please, let me go."

"I don't want you to go, baby. I want to know that when I come home, you'll be here."

"It isn't enough." She spread her hands as her voice caught, and the sound and gesture pleaded for his understanding.

He was silent a long time, looking at her. "Who would ever believe anyone so soft and sweet-looking as you could be so damned stubborn?"

She made no reply because she was fighting not to cry. If she cried, he would comfort her, and she'd be lost again.

After another long pause he said slowly, "If you must, go see your family for a week or so . . ."

Shaking her head, she replied, "That would only delay it again. I've tried every other way, but there is no solution. We have to face this. I must leave. You always find a way to postpone it, but if I leave for a while and come back, only time will pass, nothing will change or be solved. You have to let me go."

Slowly he asked, "If I agreed, what would you do?"

"Look around. Try to find something that interests me as much as your work interests you."

"I thought *I* did that." Bitterness edged into his words.

98

She just looked back at him.

"I know, I know. I'm never around. I admit it! But isn't our time together enough?"

She didn't reply. She'd already said it all.

"You're killing me. Do you realize that?" His voice was rough.

"Don't."

His head snapped around to her. "You say 'don't' to me? How can you do this to us? Am I so meaningless to you? Or do you want another man? Is that it? Kendricks is gone. Do you plan to meet him somewhere? Or, in all this time you've been lying around, doing nothing, did you find someone else?" He wrapped his hands around her shoulders but with his fury rigidly controlled he barely shook her. "Tell me, damn it!"

"You know there's no one else, Garret."

"Do I?" he lashed out, his eyes glinting fire.

"Yes."

Touched by the sheen of tears in her eyes, her soft vulnerable mouth, her fragile dearness, he released her. His body seemed to lose some vital spark. He turned from her and slumped forward with his elbows on his knees, his head down as he stared at the floor. "I don't understand you. There must be a lot of women in the world who would gladly trade places with you."

"Yes," she agreed quietly.

"But you just throw it all away. And me with it," he accused bitterly.

"Oh, Garret . . ."

"It's been really good between us. You've had everything you've wanted." Abruptly he stood and paced. Then suddenly he turned and glared at her. "All right. If that's the way you want it, it's done. I don't want an unwilling wife. Discontented and unfulfilled! Leave. Good-bye!" He stared at her, then in anguish he burst out, "Piper, *for God's sake*!" He threw out desperate hands from his sides and looked at her, then he strode to the front door, jerked it open, walked through, and slammed it shut.

She sat there, frozen. Then she heard the motor roar into life and the tires screech as the pickup roughly shot away into the night.

She sat there for a long time, feeling as if she were carved of wood. She hadn't realized how badly she would hurt him. They'd been married two years and she'd never really known him. That was terrible. Why would he care so much? How could he care when he was so seldom around her? What was it he thought he saw in her?

He didn't return.

Where was he? Back at the lab? In a wreck? Out in the desert out of gas? It was almost dawn when she slept and not long after that she wakened to toss, and then to give up and get up.

She straightened the house and changed the bed. She repacked and dressed, then she agonized over a note. She alternated between wishing he'd return and hoping he wouldn't. He didn't. It was just as well, for what else was there to say?

She removed the Do Not Disturb sign from their door and finally she drove away, east, toward "home" in central Illinois.

That night Piper called Tom from her motel. The call made him extremely uncomfortable, but he said Garret was "okay, yeah, he's okay, ya know?" Then after she got back to her parents' home in Illinois, she called Tom again. That time he'd hesitated, and she asked again, "Is he all right?" and her voice was anxious.

"Well. He's not eating good. Ya know?"

And she went around the house distracted with worry and tossed sleeplessly at night worrying about Garret . . . missing Garret.

CHAPTER FIVE

Her parents and siblings had welcomed her with affection-
ate irritation. Why would she leave such a good man?
What an idiotic thing to do! Gradually she was relegated
to a position of being both family and non-family.

It was very strange living at home again. She now
seemed out of step, like an island in a busy sea. The
"inside" family jokes had changed, and it annoyed her
that her sisters still felt free to borrow her clothes. She and
her mother exhausted each other, talking too late at night
and trying to keep each other from overdoing it. Then her
two much younger brothers vied for her attention and
quarreled because of her. She told her father, with exasperated humor, that she thought she'd run away from
home. He gave her a level look and said she'd already done
that—twice.

She stared at him. She thought that was a stunning
evaluation and wandering down to the old orchard in the
back of the house, she wondered about what he'd said.

Was it true? Had she married Garret to run away from
home and had she then run away from Garret back home?
It was a sobering thought. She remembered her parents
had tried to stop them, cautioning Piper to wait and telling
Garret not to see her until a year had passed. The lovers

would have none of that. She'd loved Garret so, and wanted so much to live with him and to be loved by him.

For a long time there in that old orchard she leaned against a low bough of one of the trees and looked at herself with a clear mind. She had been too young to marry and they hadn't known each other long enough. And she had had no idea that she'd be living in the desert. Now she knew that if she had stayed, she would have lost her sanity. But if his life had been different, if he'd had an ordinary job and she'd seen more of him, she would have stayed with him. It was true, all she had said about wanting life to have some purpose, but if he'd been with her more, it would have been enough.

She looked around the enchanted orchard and sighed. It wasn't really enchanted; it was just a bunch of old trees and weeds. Life was real, not a fairy tale.

"Tough going?" It was her father. He'd followed her down there, knowing where she'd be. Miserable, she turned to him and lay her head on his shoulder. He put a comforting hand around the back of her neck and said, "What you need is a plan."

"What sort of plan?"

"Your mother and I have been talking. The money that we had put away for your first year of school is still in the bank. You could continue the original plan and go to college. We called your Aunt Emily. She'll be in South America until August, but she would be delighted for you to stay with her. She says you can have the job with the newspaper; she checked that again. Not much of one, but you'd have some cash. She'd expect you to do your share around the house."

"But I don't know what I really want to do."

"Doing nothing won't solve anything, so take some

time and find out," Mr. Morling advised. "It's completely over with Garret?"

"Yes," she answered woefully.

"Piper, he never . . . he didn't . . . harm you, did he?"

"Oh, no! He's very sweet. It's just that I never saw him."

"Oh?" he questioned in an encouraging way.

"There has to be more to life than sitting around, or running on a treadmill to use up time and energy," Piper explained.

"You baffle me."

"Him too," she admitted.

"Well, get yourself organized."

She nodded, and they went back up the hill and down the lane to the house. And there, sitting on the front porch, was Garret! Piper turned to exchange a look of surprise with her father, but he'd left her side and was disappearing around the corner of the house. He'd known Garret was there! That's why he'd asked if Garret had ever harmed her. My God, he was there! In something of a daze she walked up the steps to the porch and she looked at him. His face was careful and guarded, his eyes watchful as he rose to greet her.

She didn't know quite what to do. Should she act angry, off-hand, or coldly courteous? While she was deciding he leaned over and kissed her so hard that he had to grab her shoulders to keep her from stumbling backward down the steps. The kiss went rippling along her nerves, causing her to tremble, and he was gratified by her response, but only his gray eyes showed that.

"What're you doing here?" she demanded coldly.

"Checking up on my wife," he said in his marvelously deep voice.

104

"Garret . . ."

"Do you know how often you just say my name? It's a compulsion when someone loves another madly."

"Gar—now listen to me. I've left you! We're separated. Go home."

"Go home? I thought this was home."

"You should leave," she groaned. "This is very embarrassing."

"Your father going to boot me out?"

"You know he likes you."

"Everyone in your family likes me except you."

"Please . . ." she implored him, a slight trace of desperation in her voice.

Then her mother was at the screen door saying, "Garret, dear," as she gave her own child a cool glance. "Would you like to wash before supper?"

"He's staying for supper?" Piper couldn't believe it.

"Well, of course!" Her mother gave her a stern frown.

Grinning a wide, pleased grin at Piper, Garret held open the screen and stood aside for her, but he couldn't resist the quick whisper, "Uh, liberated lady, is it still okay for me to hold the door for you?"

She shot him a furious look and said through her teeth, "To make such a stupid statement proves you don't understand anything I've tried to tell you!" And the smile faded from his face.

Supper was impossible. All the family chatted and laughed with Garret, who was at his most charming. Piper felt she was the outsider. Then her own mother told her to run along and pack a bag; Garret was taking her to The Lodge for the weekend!

"But . . ." she protested, shocked.

And her father said rather absently, "It'll be better than staying here. It'll give you two time to talk."

They could have no idea how Garret "talked," and how could she explain that to all of them? She pressed her lips together and replied stiffly, "I've nothing more to say."

Unfortunately Garret sighed theatrically and exclaimed that was something to be thankful for, which didn't help; then in the milling around of clearing the table and getting dishes washed and everything tidied up, no one allowed Piper anything to do.

So it wasn't long before Garret eased her out of the house, and she went woodenly. She sat in his car, stiff and silent, while Garret whistled contentedly through his teeth. He would, she mused angrily. He thought he had her right where he wanted her—a long, lustful weekend before leaving her alone again. Well, he was in for a big surprise.

The room at The Lodge was small, the one large bed almost filling it. She took a quick look and then turned baleful eyes to Garret. "I am not—" she began militantly.

"So. What're your plans? Fill me in."

He did look thinner. Maybe he wasn't eating enough. No, she reminded herself, he hadn't had that many meals at home, so it wasn't her cooking he'd missed. He'd taken off his jacket and undid his tie. She tensed. But when he unbuttoned his cuffs, he turned them back just twice. He went on. "Have you come to any decisions yet?"

Folding her arms and standing stiffly in the small floor space near the door, she replied shortly, "School."

He nodded seriously and opened his suitcase and took out her checkbook in its flowered cover, and the case with all her credit cards. "I can't imagine how you forgot these," he said, and held them out toward her.

She put her hands behind her back. "But . . ."

"You're my wife and I pay your bills."

"No."

"Yes," he stated firmly. "We'll leave it at that for the time being, Piper." He took up her purse and stuffed the two items inside. Then in a lighter vein he said, "It pleases me you'll be back in school, and I think this might be good for you. All I ask is that you find something you can do anywhere I'd be moved."

She wavered a little against his firm conviction that they were a team and both on the same side, but she said, "My parents still have the money for my first year." She watched for his reaction.

It was very serious and his level-eyed look was a little intimidating. "No. You're mine."

"Garret . . ."

"Look. Let me. I can afford to pay for your schooling. Your folks have others."

"But that has nothing to do with you."

He lifted his chin. "Don't insult me."

She was silent, her own chin stubborn. He seemed to loom in that small room. She'd forgotten how alive, how vibrant, how masculine, he was. Her intense awareness of him was shortening her breath. It was as if there were flashes of lightning that sputtered between their bodies, or touching halos of electricity. The surface of her skin became so sensitive that she was extremely conscious of the feel of her clothes covering her body.

She knew he was watching her. Nervously she licked her lips, then shot him an alarmed glance. He grinned and held out his arms. "Come here."

She couldn't know how she affected him. She was standing there so straight and brave, with such large, darkened

107

eyes. She was so dear to him. His body had never forgotten the impact of her, and the tingling inside him increased. He waited. "Are you shy with me, Piper?" His voice was very tender.

She felt her face flush, but it was the tears starting that she didn't understand. "I feel as if I've been thrown to the lions . . . lion."

He came the few steps to her, a low rumbling in his throat. He leaned and teasingly gave her cheek a chaste kiss. "Want me to sleep on the couch?" There was, of course, no couch. There wasn't even enough room for him to sleep on the floor. And it annoyed her that she should feel so awkward with him.

She looked at him, forgetting herself. She saw not only the height and breadth of him, the ease and grace of his movements, but his rumpled hair and his tired face. He must have driven straight through, just to see her. Her hungry eyes drank in the sight of him and she knew she loved him, she desired him; she always had and she probably always would.

Blushing a little, she went to him and threw herself into his quickly opened arms against his hard body and stood pressed close to him, relishing the feel of him. "Oh, Garret." She lifted her head back for his kiss, and he groaned against her mouth. She wiggled, trying to get even closer, and he helped her do that by crushing her in his arms . . . and she couldn't breathe.

Apparently he realized it, and interrupted the kiss so she could gasp some air. But then his kisses deepened, his arms moved, and she began to squirm in minute movements, and he groaned again. The backs of her knees tingled. He loosened his smothering embrace, and her hand went to his shirt buttons as she admitted in a whisper, "I want you."

He murmured, "It's about time" as he pulled her tightly back against him and began to kiss her deeper and deeper. Her blood sang through her body and her bones melted as she gasped and clutched him closer.

She'd thought she'd never be with him again, yet he was miraculously there with her. Her fingers worked at his shirt as if fighting against the strong material. He was real and he was there! His arms were around her and his body was pressing into hers; and those were his hands that moved on her, stroking loving paths over her shoulders, along the sides of her breasts, down her back, and cupping her buttocks to pull her tightly against him.

She had help as he wrenched out of his shirt. He then took the bottom of hers and simply snapped it apart. She heard buttons ping briefly against the wall and one rolled on the floor somewhere, but he'd grabbed her back against him, and her senses were suffused with the sensation of her skin and nipples against his hair-textured chest and his hard muscles flattening her softness against his rock-hard surface.

The rest of their clothes were thrown aside, the discarding only a brief distraction as their struggle continued. Their need raged through their bodies and clamored for release, their greedy hands and eager mouths in frenzied action.

Piper climbed quickly backward onto the bed, pulling Garret down after her. He lay on her, glorying in the feel of her there where he wanted her, then she opened to him and he took her. Their bodies fused in the torch of their hot passion, and their frantic hunger drove them to a raging climax—to a roaring, writhing relief.

* * *

It was a long time before they spoke. She'd been so wild she felt embarrassed, but she'd missed him so badly. "I can't believe I've behaved so . . . so . . ."

He smoothed her damp hair back from her face. "You're married to me, and it was magnificent. I've missed you like bloody hell."

Her hands slowly wandered over his sweaty face and shoulders as they soothed him and took pleasure in touching him. "How could you miss a bloody hell?"

"That's how I've felt without you."

"Well, it has been three weeks . . ."

"I had the blond wig, but I needed you under it."

"You knew!" she accused.

Astonished she'd ask, he replied, "Well, of course!"

She pretended to pull his hair and shook his head doing it, but then he snuggled into her neck and made her squeal. He kissed her tenderly and gently rubbed his whiskers along her cheek and throat and breathed in her scent. After a time he leaned on an elbow and looked at her. She smiled just a little, staring back.

She was there. She'd just made wild love to him and she cared about him. His voice was husky with emotion. "I kept thinking you'd . . . maybe, well, write to me."

She admitted, "I must have written you a hundred letters."

"Oh, baby, why didn't you send them all?"

"But it was all the same old things. We've been over it all so many times."

"I've agreed to you going back to school. It'll kill me to have you gone from me, but I have agreed. You did think of me? Did you miss me?"

"I have for two years."

110

He ignored that stinging barb and went on. "Tom told me you'd called him."

She roused, huffy with indignation. "He swore on his mother's grave!"

Garret chuckled. "He told me how you'd made him swear." He had to stop talking in order to kiss her lovingly. "He said that it didn't count because he doesn't have a mother."

"But he has . . ."

"He said as long as he can remember, his mother has said to him, 'You're no son of mine!' " He went on. "Why didn't you want me to know you'd called about me?"

"We're separated."

He pulled her soft body against his hard length.

"I mean . . . well, I left you," she added.

"But you worried about me," he reminded her.

"You'd been so upset."

"Well, hell yes," he huffed. "Who wouldn't be?"

"Why did you come, Garret? You know it solves nothing."

"It solves one or two things, and, anyway, you didn't have your checkbook and your dad said . . ."

"Dad? When did you talk to him?"

"Just about every day."

"He never even mentioned it!" she exclaimed.

"I told him not to."

"And I suppose he swore on Grandma's grave . . ."

"No, I told him I'd lop off his bloody head."

"You didn't!" she gasped.

"Lop it off? No, but then he didn't tell you either."

"He did ask if you'd ever harmed me."

"Yes." Garret nodded. "I can see how he would."

111

There was a brief silence as she waited, then she asked, "Don't you want to know what I said?"

"No need. I know that I haven't, and I know you would say that I hadn't."

"I wish I didn't love you," she said with such deep pain.

"Oh, Piper . . ." He pulled her close to him, and then he said, "You're lucky you do love me, you obstinate little wretch, because you're going to spend the rest of your life with me."

"Garret, we're separated!"

"Don't kid yourself."

They spent an idyllic, magical three days together. And once they talked about their courtship. He said, "All I remember about that whole time was plotting how to get your gorgeous body." When that made her blush, he asked curiously, "Now why does that make you blush? An old married woman like you?" He was amused. "I've already devoted two days to trying to quench your lusts, and you've been eager help."

"Well, you see, I knew what you were doing, and I was having trouble not helping you do it."

"I believe we had a communication problem."

She looked at him suddenly somber and said, "We still do."

He touched her cheek. "Anything is solvable."

"You shouldn't have come here," she said softly.

"Now, don't tell me how miserable I've made you."

"You have . . ."

He warned, "Piper!"

But she went on. "You've shown me what it was like when we met. I hadn't dreamed it. It's exactly the way I remembered . . . only it's better."

"See? Come home with me."

112

She looked at him with helpless sadness. "I'm going to cry."

He replied grimly, "I'll join you."

"If I went home with you, you'd try to remember to come home on time, then you'd be a little late, and as I'd warm your supper, you'd say, 'Oh, I grabbed a sandwich.' Then you'd feel bad and you'd take me to bed and be really wonderful to me. After that you'd call to say you'd been delayed. Then you'd forget to call, and finally you'd either drag in and just go to sleep, or you'd make love to me and then go to sleep." They were quiet before she added, "It'd be just like before."

There was no denying what she said. After a while he asked if her car was working all right. Piper said it was. Then she asked, "What time do you have to leave tomorrow?"

He heard the "have to." "Not until evening. Are you free all day?"

"Oh, yes."

His bruised heart heard the quick, certain reply. What was he to do? He couldn't let her go. He couldn't lose her. He tried to see what was in store for them, and he couldn't.

The next day, as they walked downtown in Springfield, Piper asked, "When it's . . . over . . . between us, will you call Barb Tallman again?"

"How can you think it's ever going to be over for us?" Garret took her hand and his fingers felt the presence of the wedding ring. "You're mine for all time. Can't you feel that?"

She could . . . when he was there beside her. But she only looked up at him and her eyes were bleak, for she knew he would be leaving.

113

* * *

The next day was typical for Illinois in August, with the intense humidity and the temperature equally oppressive. They spent most of their last day in bed with the air-conditioner on high. Garret commented that it was too bad he could not take some of the excess moisture back to the desert with him. Piper told him about a PBS special she'd seen on Egypt and how water wasn't the solution to arid areas, that water just brought salt to the surface, which killed any living plant, that the need was for plants that could live with little or no moisture. That led to the use of oil sludge to hold sand in place until plants could take hold and grow roots.

And they talked. It was something they'd never really done. It was new territory to be explored with pleasure and some surprise. It was actually the beginning of their knowing each other: a post-marriage courtship.

They had a difficult time parting. She cried, which put him through a wringer. He asked her again to go home with him, but that only made her cry harder. He finally drew an uneven breath, kissed her yet again, got into his car, and drove away.

She sat on the porch swing in the purple twilight for a long lonely time. He'd had his lustful weekend, and he'd left her alone again.

Her family avoided her. For the next several days they treated her to forbearing glances and exasperated sighs. Her brothers asked when Garret was coming back. Her father shook his head impatiently at her, and both her sisters mentioned she was a moron.

She told her mother she felt forlorn and abandoned. Her mother replied unhelpfully that when it comes to the bottom line we all have to live our lives pretty much alone, that life was a series of endless compromises, that we each have to make our own decisions or try to survive under someone else's, that Garret was a superior catch, and she'd best not do anything unsalvageably stupid. Piper began to sympathize with the Bible's frozen snake who bit the man who warmed it.

When it came time to move east across the state to her aunt's house at Champaign-Urbana, her sisters were gleeful in reclaiming closet space, but mourned the loss of her car. Her brothers hugged her, surprised it was almost time for their school to start too. Her father wiped his eyes and blew his nose, and her mother frowned, hugged her quite abruptly, and told her to get along and not to prolong the good-byes. So she knew they all loved her.

Emily was her father's older sister, and certainly nothing like her brother. Piper's father always said he was five feet nine inches, but the ninth inch was seven-eighths short.

Emily really was five feet nine inches and she was fifty-two the year Piper moved in with her. She had a superb figure and her hair would have been salt and pepper, but she rinsed the white strands a light brown and the effect was smashing.

She'd never married, she had acquaintances nationwide, her wit was subtle, and her mind was like a steel trap. She could be startlingly abrupt.

She taught contracts in the School of Law at the University of Illinois, and it was rumored she'd take a lover from among the best of the senior class and had for the last twenty years.

Her house, four blocks away on the Urbana side of the

115

campus, was large, old-fashioned, and filled with antiques. Almost every room had a fireplace and the roof was clustered with chimney pots.

She welcomed Piper without the usual physical demonstrations and glad cries. After she showed Piper which room would be hers, she listened to why Piper had left her husband. She gave no sign of approval or disapproval at all, but she did understand. That almost dissolved Piper into tears because Emily was the first who hadn't thought her an idiot.

After advising that when she lived in the desert Piper could have typed books for the blind and investigated a choice of splendid correspondence schools, Emily suggested she go the regular route of freshman classes. But Piper thought she ought to audit a mixture. Emily cautioned against that. Piper should study for credit so she wouldn't lose any while deciding what field she wanted.

So Piper chose classes in journalism with studio art and cooking on the side. Emily looked at the schedule with a frown, unable to understand Piper's lack of direction. "Apparently what does interest you is a hodgepodge and typically female." She shook her head; for Emily there'd never been any hesitation or doubt. "At least they're all in the School of Arts and Sciences. Why not audit a class in law? It might grab you." But even saying it, Emily knew it was a waste of time suggesting it.

Piper confirmed that. "Ever since I read that Justice Oliver Wendell Holmes said if you were able to eat a pound of sawdust without butter you could learn the law, somehow it seemed a dry subject to me." Emily didn't pretend she'd never heard that.

Garret insisted on paying Emily what it would have cost for Piper to stay in the dorm, and Piper went personally to decline the newspaper job that Emily had set up for her.

The first week of classes was interesting, and being older made her more discerning about her teachers. For instance, one art professor's lectures were so dry and his eyes so dull and dead that she switched from that course to a painting class. And that's how she met Professor B.C.

He looked like Bill Cosby, so the students dubbed him Professor B.C., and occasionally he'd ham it up and mimic the man he looked like. He was an easy teacher, patient and encouraging. He told Piper to stop copying and do her own pictures—dream them, imagine them, do something she cared about so she'd love the lines and the subject. And she timidly began to take his advice.

Their first assignment had been an object. The second was a single-person-interior. She wondered what in the world to paint, but lying in bed that night in agony over missing Garret she knew she would do it of him leaning in bed, looking down at her.

When Emily realized Piper needed a room in which to paint, she cleared out a small storage room off the upstairs bath. There were exposed pipes along one wall and a bare floor, so nothing could be harmed, and there was only one window, but it did face the constant northern light. There Piper set up her easel and began on her painting of Garret. The face came quite well, and she consulted pictures she had of him to make minor corrections. But it was the body that baffled her.

The one male nude they had for figure drawing was too old, his muscles soft sagging. She walked the campus and studied different men's bodies. There was one man she'd noticed. His face was nothing like Garret's, but the body . . . ah, the body. She wondered what he looked like

117

without his clothes. At breakfast she told Emily she felt like a dirty old woman.

Emily advised, "Be businesslike when you ask him to pose, and pay the regular fee. Ask your prof's permission and work in a studio at school. You'd be indiscreet if you brought him home; he might get the wrong idea."

The next time Piper saw him he was with several other men, and he looked back at her. She strode forward, brisk and businesslike. She asked if she might speak to him. He grinned widely and agreed, and the other two chuckled and protested, what about them? She ignored them, but they listened.

She began confidently. "I'm Piper Raymond . . ."

"Well, hello there . . ." All three crowded closer. "Piper, huh?" They were cheerful and amused.

". . . and I wondered if you'd consider posing for me? I am . . ."

"Absolutely!" He immediately dropped his books, stepped on the back of each shoe, kicking them off, as he skimmed out of his T-shirt!

"Wait!" she shouted in panic. "Not here!"

"Your place or mine?" He was enjoying himself enormously as he played up to his companions' delighted laughter and comments.

She turned and fled, although they called and shouted for her to wait. One needed cooperation to be businesslike.

So she abandoned Garret's painting temporarily and did a self-portrait that showed her standing in her bare little studio. She'd captured her solemn face very well; she painted the hair flowing and free, her jeans and short-sleeve shirt were dabbed in shades of blue, and her ankles were entrapped in a drift of sand. The pipes were elaborated into a puzzle that showed her own confusion. The

118

window showed a frame of bars opened back against the side of the wall with the window hinged open to the other side, and through it was the open air, a bird, a part of a tree and, faintly, faraway clouds.

In the upper corner to the left was a spider web, with a vibrant heart captured there, and the spider watched the artist with binoculars. The bottom of the web was torn, with one strand clinging to Piper's right arm; that hand held her paintbrush. Her other held a letter—a letter she had received from Garret.

He'd written, pouring out questions, telling her about the sun on the sand, the emptiness of the house, his bed, his arms. His attempts at cooking had been almost satisfactory, but one ingredient was always missing: It was she.

Emotion brimming, she'd called him, but there'd been no answer. He had probably been at the lab. She'd put the ringing phone back into its cradle with the familiar feeling of isolation.

In her short story writing class, Piper learned that her professor had an interest in graphology when all of the students were asked to write their signatures on the piece of paper being passed around. When she handed the paper to the young woman sitting next to her, Piper couldn't help but notice how exotic-looking she was. But upon examining her more closely, Piper realized it was a calculated façade. Her ears were double-pierced with tiny diamonds in the upper holes and tiny loops in the lower ones. Her hair was long, the crown wrapped like an Arab's headpiece, the ends tied at the back of her head disappearing into the rest of her loose brown mane. Her makeup was skillfully done, the colors perfectly complementing her olive skin.

Her name was Sara Jenkins. It should have been Sara Wanderer, or Sara Shalimar, Piper thought as she looked at the paper the young woman passed back to her. She had written her name two lines high on the paper with a flourish. She took the paper back from Piper's hands and studied Piper's signature, her head slightly aslant, before she smiled with great charm.

So it wasn't Piper who made the friend, it was Sara who chose her, Sara who allowed the friendship. It was undemanding, no female chats, confidences, or talk of men, just an easy companionship.

During the last days of summer they met for sack lunches on the shady side of the campus lawn. They took in the free string quartet concerts at the music center, and they walked through the first student monthly art show where Piper had two pictures hanging—a drawing of a picnic and a sleeping cat. Sara looked at them carefully. Piper sneaked quick looks at her face, so she saw Sara push out her lower lip and give an absent nod of approval.

With the football season and the freshmen in the fraternities chanting the obligatory pep songs, Piper marked the leaves on the trees turning to shades of red.

Piper missed Garret almost with a sickness. One day as she was out walking, thinking deeply about him, her way was blocked by the man with Garret's body. As she dropped her eyes and moved to walk around him, he stopped her, grinning. "Hey. I'm sorry I botched it. Will you give me a second chance?"

"I was serious. I'd like you to pose at the art school for the regular fee."

He hesitated, looking at her, then asked, "Naked?"

She turned around to walk away, but again he stopped

her. "Wait. Look. Nobody's ever asked me to do anything quite like this. I'm not sure I know how to handle it. But I'd like to see you again."

"I'm married." She said it formally, her lips thin. "Somehow I've given you the wrong idea."

"No, you haven't." He hurried to placate her. "You want me to pose for you. Okay? I'll do it. When?"

"My professor said I could use a studio Saturday mornings from eight to ten." She was still a little doubtful.

He cautioned, "I'm not too bright in the morning."

"That's okay. I just want to paint your . . . well, I just need to . . ." She blushed. "In swim trunks!"

He grinned with amusement and returning confidence. "Okay. Where's the studio? I'll be there."

She told him. He nodded, writing it in his notebook, and repeated, "Eight Saturday morning. My God, I'll have to get up at ten till!" With a rueful shake of his head, he started away.

"Oh," she called. "What's your name?"

"Bingham," he shouted back. "Reginald Bingham IV."

At supper she reported to Emily and added, "I wonder if his mother knows he's posing for a strange woman."

"I know his father. Nice family. But this is Reg's third university."

"What's the trouble?"

"About like you—no goals," Emily replied. "Naldie, his dad, says if kidnaping weren't such a threat, Reg should take a trip to Europe until he matures and settles down a little."

"Lots of money," Piper guessed.

"Lots and lots."

"Siblings?"

"Just Reg."

On Saturday at eight o'clock, in jeans, paint smock, with no makeup and her hair in a topknot, Piper was in the designated studio with her equipment ready when Reg arrived. Piper showed him where to change and went back to squeezing pigment onto her white tray and mixing flesh colors as she waited for him.

He felt awkward in the abbreviated suit and hesitated, barefooted, in the doorway. He shifted his weight on one leg, standing in a parody of relaxed indifference.

"Oh, hi." She was total business. "Get up here, sit down, and place yourself like this." She hoisted herself up on the platform, sat with her back to the easel, curled her body forward with her legs bent carelessly, then she turned her shoulders partly so that her face looked down around her shoulder. He watched her. She looked up at him inquiringly. "See?"

He took her place. She reached to move his shoulders, then bit her lower lip in concentration and jumped down from the platform to study him. "Put your left hand higher on your thigh. Right. We'll do fifteen minutes, then a five-minute break. If you get tired, tell me."

"You're really going to paint me?"

She looked blank. "Of course."

"Oh."

She didn't inquire what he'd anticipated, but stood looking at him. He began to fidget, and he moved his hands restlessly on his thighs.

She questioned, "Is the position uncomfortable for you?"

"No. No." He shook his head.

"Bend your body forward just about two inches. There!

122

Bring your left thumb to where your thigh meets your body. Look down at me. Right. Perfect." She adjusted the lights, then sat down so that her head was only just above the surface of the platform. It was the angle she wanted. Then she studied him.

He coughed self-consciously and said in a husky voice, "Don't look at me that way."

Her mind snapped back from her intense concentration and she said impatiently, "I've got to look at you if I'm going to paint you."

After a little longer he said, "Do you have any idea what that does to a guy to have a girl eye him like that?"

Annoyed, she said in bursts, "I'm an old married woman. Forget me. Be detached."

It was easier when she took up her brushes and began to paint. She told him to look around where he chose; she'd tell him when to look back at her. She worked quickly with sure strokes, her concentration complete. For her the time passed with astonishing speed, but he watched the clock. She painted through his breaks, but she said he could not watch her nor could he see the painting until it was done. That made him grumble.

There had been people in the halls, sounds in the building, and Professor B.C. had looked in a couple of times checking up on them, and once he'd entered to observe.

When the two hours were up, Reg dressed and returned to invite her for coffee. She declined absently, and he scowled at her until he understood she didn't realize he hadn't left. When he did, he closed the door quietly behind him.

The next Saturday she brought a tape recorder and cassettes from Books on Tape. She knew that Reg had

123

been in the area described on the tape and figured he might enjoy reliving his own adventure.

Sara came in for a while and sat in a corner, watching and listening, then she left. That morning passed quickly for Piper.

It was Indian summer. The days were glorious, warm, and lazy; the nights were crisp and fall's special fragrance was in the air. Light wools were being worn, and the fireplaces were used more and the smell of burning wood filtered through the air. It was the time for hot apple cider with cinnamon stick swirls and fresh doughnuts.

In her little studio Piper lovingly worked on Garret's picture. It wasn't quite right. It was Garret, but there wasn't that special look that he had when he looked at her lying next to him in bed. That was what she wanted.

So on the third Saturday, with Reg up on the platform, she touched in a highlight here, a shadow there. She squinted at it and thought it was perfect. But what was lacking? She focused on Reg, who was listening to another Book on Tape. She was reluctant to initiate such a conversation, but finally she asked, "Reg, look at me as if I were someone you cared about who was lying next to you on a bed."

His first reaction was surprise, then came a big grin and a leer that made her angry. "I'm serious. Can't you look that way? Quit clowning." When he looked startled, and she considered all the play of emotions and expressions that had just crossed his face, she snapped, directing him, "Think of a girl. Now think of looking around while you're sitting on her bed and she is lying there wanting you."

His eyes grazed over her body and came back to her

face. There was the appreciation, the hunger, the anticipation . . . and the rising desire.

"Hold it!" Quickly she narrowed Garret's painted eyes, parted his lips and made the lower one fuller. It was what she'd wanted. She stepped back saying, "It's finished."

His voice husky, he replied, "I think I am too."

"You can see it now," Piper said, not actually thinking about him.

"Why don't you come up here with me?"

"Cut that out, Reg." She frowned briefly in exasperation. Then with a tiny brush she delicately touched the eye on the painting, stood back and squinted her eyes, going closer, then moving back again.

When he approached her he was dressed, his jacket casually hooked over his shoulder on one finger; the other hand was in his trouser pocket. He came beside her and finally saw the picture. First he exclaimed, "You made me blond!" Then he looked closer and frowned. "That's not me."

"It's my husband."

He asked, "Divorced? Separated?"

"While he's out west, I'm here in school."

"He probably has no idea how to satisfy your needs."

"Good God, Reg!" she exclaimed in irritation.

Sara, knowing it was to be a short final session, sauntered casually into the room and joined them viewing the finished painting. What had seemed a pillow in the lower left corner had become a woman's dark head, the shadows were her spilled hair being lifted in a very provocative way by her almost obscured fingers. And the rumpled bedcovers were the only indication of her relaxed body.

Sara commented, "That's the most sensuous picture

since the one of Rudolf Nureyev and Michelle Phillips advertising their film, *Valentino.*"

Modestly, Reg interposed, "I was the model."

Professor B.C. came in, having heard their voices, and nodded his head twice. Then he said, "How about a little more shadow here; a touch stronger highlight there?" It pleased him that Piper didn't automatically obey, but examined his suggestions before following his directions.

Then she asked, "Do you think it's too intimate?"

He shook his head. "No, it's beautiful. Only a woman who loved a man could see him that way and then paint it."

Reg interrupted, "She used me." Then he frowned at his own words.

CHAPTER SIX

When Piper's picture of Garret was dry enough to transport, she brought it home, carrying it across the campus—wrapped. She felt a little self-conscious about it because of the comments from Sara, Reg, and Professor B.C., so she hadn't shown it to anyone else. She smuggled it past Emily and upstairs to her room to hang it across from her bed. It didn't help her to sleep.

Then Garret called her and said he thought of her so constantly that it was interfering with his work. She doubted that. He said he'd been giving a lot of thought to her discontent, and he'd done some research on women and found the busiest ones were those who had gardens and ground their own grains.

"Are you trying to turn *me* into a farmer?"

"No, no, I'm only trying to find a way to get you back with me. I'm just losing my mind and working too hard." She made a rude sound, which he ignored. "I'm flying up for the weekend if it's okay with you."

"Oh, Garret . . ." She was pleased and surprised that he had considered her feelings. After they'd hung up, she began to plan meals, and then baked for three days. Emily asked her to stop or she'd have to buy a freezer. But Piper

127

only said, "If he flies in, he should get here Friday night!" And she walked around in a dreamlike state.

She rushed home from class on Friday morning and met Emily, who was coming out the front door. Her aunt smiled a puzzling smile and said, "I wish he was ten years older," as she crossed the wide porch and went down the steps.

"Who?" Piper asked.

"Garret."

"Then he'd be forty."

Emily turned her head back to show Piper a wicked smile and, with a provocative swish of her body, she said in a smoky voice, "That's close enough."

Piper smiled and chided, "Emily!" Then her face went blank and her mouth opened and she whirled toward the door just as a large hand reached out, took her arm, pulled her inside, and she squealed in surprise. Garret closed the door after her and enveloped her in his arms.

"What . . ." she began, and when he let her up for air, she added, ". . . are you doing . . ." and she continued, ". . . here so soon?"

"You have a talent for the most unwelcoming statements." But it didn't seem to bother him.

After a few minutes, when her body had been caressed and stroked into a state of perfect contentment by his strong hands, and her face was delightfully reddened, she sighed, leaning against him. "There just isn't any substitute for whiskers."

She was relaxed and happy, but his muscles were as taut and tense as they could be. His voice ragged, he whispered, "Let's go to your room."

She was scandalized. "We can't do that!"

"Emily already showed me the way, and my suitcase is

there." By the time he had hustled her halfway up the stairs—and she remembered the painting of him at the bottom of her bed!

It's one thing to lust for a man, but it's entirely different to be so blatant about it, she thought. She could have died. Her face flamed, and she swallowed loudly.

"What's the matter?" He was very amused. His gray eyes glittered as he gazed at her.

"Uh . . ."

"You're not harboring another . . . man up there, are you?"

He'd already seen the picture. She knew he had. Was he shocked? She'd been so caught up in thinking about him, she'd forgotten it. Why hadn't she put it in her studio as soon as she'd heard he was coming? "Garret . . ." Her eyes turned up to his face painfully. He looked smug. Yes, he'd certainly seen the picture. And he was pleased!

"I think it's great!" He laughed.

"Why, Garret!"

By that time he had guided her to the door to her bedroom and flung it open. He scooped her up, and she felt stiff as a board. He carried her in and kicked the door shut.

With her still in his arms he stood in front of the painting, and really looked at it. "It's good." He continued to move his eyes over it. "I wish you'd painted it from the angle behind my head so that it would be of you lying there, looking up at me, your eyes shadowed with desire, your mouth soft, inviting my kisses, your arms up like that, your body waiting for me, longing for me." He leaned down and kissed her with such tenderness that her bones melted and she became a little dizzy. His voice purred, "Ah, baby girl, did you miss me?"

How could he doubt it? With that picture of him at the foot of her bed? "Well, I have been very busy . . ."

"You wretch!" He tossed her in a bounce onto the high bed and began to take off his clothes.

Her mouth parted as she watched him, her face soft and vulnerable as thrills coursed through her body. He was there. He was actually there in her room. "Oh, Garret . . ." He finished undressing quickly, and she stared at his body with new appreciation. The symmetry, the planes, the flow of muscles rolling under his tanned flesh, his manliness, his obvious virility—him! And her blood ran hot, flushing her skin, and the surface of her body prickled with excitement.

Tossing aside the last of his clothes, he untied her Nikes and peeled off her golf socks. He undid her jeans, pushed her backward, took hold of the bottoms of the pant legs, and jounced her out of them.

"Garret . . ."

But then he crawled up on the bed, on top of her, and bent to kiss her.

"I can't breathe," she gasped.

"Oh, do it later," he replied, but he slid partly off her so that his hands could move up under her flannel shirt to smooth her naked stomach, then to move up over her round breasts to tease and stroke and knead them.

She undid her buttons, and he spread the shirt to look at her. His voice deep and husky, he said, "You have to repaint that picture. You are a thing of beauty." And, following his hands, his mouth caressed her lovingly. Against her stomach his low voice roughened. He whispered, "Oh, my love, I've missed you so."

Running eager hands into his hair, she replied with a gulp. "Oh, Garret . . ." But he moved up to tease her

130

mouth open so that his kiss was full and loving. The slow rising licking of desire wakened in the pit of her stomach.

Against her throat he muttered, "I dream about you in the night." His mouth on her shoulder, he ran his tongue along her skin in lazy, tasting circles. Then he moved to her ear to breathe gently there, to allow his tongue to explore its shell, flooding her with overwhelming desire. The satin tips of her breasts responded to his tongue and his hand as he caressed the skin of her inner thighs. He ran his fingertips up along her stomach and spread his hot hand over her lovely breasts, caressing them and squeezing them as he felt their fullness.

He lay back and paused to look at her. His eyes flaming embers, his hair rumpled from her fingers, he smiled at her. She couldn't take her hands from him. Her lips were parted by her breathing, by her desire. They were soft and inviting and her hands massaged his shoulders and gently pressed him toward her.

"I love you, Piper." His voice rumbled in his chest as he leaned over her and kissed her again. But with that kiss all his restraints weakened. He rolled on top of her and eased into her, then he rocked them as he forced his hands under her to cup her buttocks closer to him, and he touched the deepest recesses of her body, making her feel intensely sensual and beautifully complete. Their passion rose, carrying them to dizzying heights of ecstasy, and they groaned and gasped in the agony of their love as together they reached that sweet release.

She left him sleeping in her bed. There wasn't anything close to a direct flight out of the desert, so he'd been traveling and had been stuck in airports most of the night. As he'd sighed contentedly into sleep, she watched him, her heart filled with him, her body gratified by his. He was there. He was in her room. He was with her.

Distracted, she went to the kitchen to fix lunch and to figure out what to prepare for dinner. Then, after he'd slept about an hour, she carried a tray up to the bedroom. But he was not there; she found him standing in her studio staring at her self-portrait. His face was serious as he raised his eyes and looked steadily at her. But he made no comment. Then he took the tray from her and they went downstairs to eat.

Emily returned for supper. She appreciated the food, but the other two were hardly aware of what went into their mouths. They left Emily, whose turn it was to clear away after the meal, and they went out to walk in the moonlight along the campus, holding hands and talking about unimportant things.

Finally he asked her, "Do you really think of me as a spider?" The image in her self-portrait had really disturbed him.

To keep the conversation light, she replied, "Completely. Big and hairy, with lots of hands."

He leaned her against a tree in the dark, pinning her there with his hard body. "Spiders have feet, not hands." He kissed her an uncountable number of times. Then he suggested, "Let's go back to your room. I never knew it could be so much fun, moving in with a coed. My own college years weren't this interesting."

"Really?"

He kissed her again, then sighed. "It's very difficult having you away from me."

"Me too." She took his hand, and they walked along, not talking, just being together.

*　*　*

The next morning, Saturday, Piper took Garret to the art school so he could meet Professor B.C., and later Garret met Sara and Reg. The two couples walked in the bright sunlight, kicking the fallen leaves and talking.

Sara looked at Garret and studied him, weighing him, just as Professor B.C. had done. Reg too was curious, examining Garret carefully through eyes a trifle narrowed.

Feeling secure with Piper, Garret was amused by Reg and was therefore kind to him. They went for hamburgers and decided to go to the football game. Afterward they all went back to Emily's, but she was gone for the evening. So they thawed steaks and chose which of the frozen baked goods to sample. Garret and Reg went for wine, using Piper's car. They built a fire in the fireplace after dinner and talked on into the night. Finally Reg and Sara went off, leaving Piper and Garret to go to bed, to make love sleepily and fall into a dreamless sleep.

They wakened late on Sunday. Piper went to fetch the paper, set aside by Emily, who'd gone to church, and they read in bed, then lay in each other's arms talking, their eyes moving constantly, each one studying the other.

The day was gray and chilly and they wore heavier clothes when they went out that afternoon to walk, engrossed in each other, oblivious to the rest of the world. Piper said rather mournfully, "I wish you would quit your job and move to Urbana."

"I gave that serious thought, Piper, but I can't. My job is important to me, and I want it and you."

She took his arm in both her hands and pulled it back against her breasts, laying her head on his shoulder. And that night their lovemaking was filled with tender poignancy. She said, "I don't want you to leave."

"Nor do I."

"I love you." Her voice quavered.

"But not enough."

"Oh, Garret . . ."

"You say 'Oh, Garret' in the most diverse ways."

"But you are diverse."

"I'm a simple man. All I want is my wife, a job I like, and a home with children."

"Then do you want a divorce?"

He denied that. "Not so far."

"Do you love me?"

"Need you ask?"

She was mournful. "Apparently I do."

"I'm out of my mind with love for you. It makes me sick you're not with me. I ache for you, and groan in my sleep, and reach for you. I catch a faint whiff of something, and I'm flooded with the need of seeing you, touching you. I feel as if I've been cut in half."

She started to cry. He comforted her with a heart-wrenching tenderness. She wakened in the morning with a headache, puffy eyes, and a red nose. He said she looked gorgeous. She knew he did. She helped him pack after breakfast and sniffed around, blowing her nose.

Seeing their misery, Emily said good-bye, shaking her head over them impatiently. And Piper drove him to the airport.

With Garret gone again, Piper was assailed by the familiar emptiness, the loneliness. Even so, she drove home agonizing over what she was doing to them. Any woman would want Garret and be contented just to have him. Outside of Emily, no one she knew had any under-standing of her wanting more out of life. Was she so different from other women?

As she opened the front door, she remembered that Garret had studied her self-portrait very intensely. She went upstairs to her studio to try to see the painting with his eyes—but it was gone! It had been taken from the wooden stretchers.

Quick glances showed the other paintings were still there, then, in a panic, she ran to her room, but the picture of Garret had not been taken. She ran down the stairs to the study calling, "Emily!"

Emily glanced up at Piper over her glasses. "You survived the parting?"

"Almost. Did you see the painting I did of me?"

"Obviously it isn't in your studio." Emily guessed that.

"It's gone! Who? Do you suppose Garret could have taken it?"

"It wouldn't particularly surprise me." Emily shrugged.

But the thought astonished Piper, and when he called to say he'd arrived back at the compound, she asked, "Did you take the picture of me?"

His reply was off-handed. "Yeah."

It still surprised her. "Why?"

"It'll help me. I'll look at it and maybe it'll help me try to be patient about your fling."

With indignation she yelled, *"Fling?"* Her eyes flared at the blameless wall.

His voice placid, he replied, "Umm-hmm."

"Garret . . ."

"I love you, baby. It was a miracle to be with you. I wish you were here right now. I'd wrap my arms around you and . . . sleep a week! You wore me out."

The next day Professor B.C. advised Piper, "Don't let that man of yours on too long a leash, child, or you might

135

lose him." That made her uneasy. Then Sara said, "He's a treasure. I hope you've a strong lock on his box. Some treasure-hunting woman might just try to snatch him." That caused her uneasiness to spill over into alarm.

When she saw Reg, he watched her for a minute then said, "You used me as a sculptor would use an armature. I was the pipe and wire and wooden holds for the clay of Garret."

She nodded, thinking he understood.

"I don't like being any man's substitute!" He took her shoulders in a bruising grip and kissed her brutally. He raised his head to look stormily at her, then leaned over and deliberately ran his tongue over her bottom lip. "I'm my own man. I stand alone. And no woman mistakes or substitutes me for another man." Then he turned and strode angrily away.

It shocked her because even with her body sated from her weekend with Garret she had felt kindled by Reg's furious kiss. If she could feel an attraction to another man, couldn't Garret be aroused by another woman? She had assumed he'd been faithful. But had he been? She was separated from him. And women were bold and aggressive. Would Garret be enticed by another woman? And because another man had caused her to spark, jealousy over Garret was hatched and lived in her.

When Garret called her the next week, she blundered around verbally then blurted out, "Have you been faithful to me?"

He chuckled lazily in her ear. "I haven't the strength not to be."

"Do you look at other women?" she asked the man she had discarded.

"Here?" He was incredulous. "I sleep with a blond wig. It's all there is around here to attract me."

"Garret . . ."

"My picture still there?"

"Oh, yes."

He groaned. "I wish to God I was."

"Me too."

"Give Sara my love, tell Emily I wish I was thirty years older. And watch out for Reg. He's young, but he has good taste and he may very well have a yen for you. Keep out of his clutches."

"I will," she promised in a distracted way.

"Just see to it that you behave yourself."

"You too." Her voice was a little sharp.

He laughed, and after they hung up she dwelt on that laugh. What had it meant?

She told Emily about Garret wishing he was thirty years older, and Emily agreed. "Especially after seeing that painting you did of him in bed. My God."

"Why, Emily!" Piper gasped in an annoyed way.

But Emily only laughed and cleared the table.

So Piper censored his greeting to Sara. "He said to give you his . . . hello."

Sara smiled, secretly amused, and thanked her. Piper's bristles were showing.

Piper had visited her family once that fall, but had been restless to get back to her studio. Her letters to her family had shortened to notes, she was so busy. She still wrote to Garret, but instead of writing in reply, he'd been calling her every Thursday at eight in the evening. She'd tried to call him several times, but there was never an answer.

She'd called Tom once and asked where Garret was. He'd said at the lab, probably, and his voice had been guileless. He offered to go over to the lab and find him. But she said never mind. Then when she'd told Tom to give Garret her love, he'd suggested she do that herself. And he'd sounded gratingly critical.

Piper threw herself into her classes. One short story she wrote received special praise and the suggestion to enter it in a competition. Impulsively she did an illustration for it, and Professor B.C. was pleased.

Piper didn't go home at Thanksgiving, but stayed with Emily. The campus was empty and quiet. She was working in a studio at the art school on her share of a group project when Reg walked in.

She hadn't expected to see anyone. "You still around?"

"You could sound more welcoming than that!"

"Greetings! How nice to see you?" She smiled, choosing to forget their last meeting and his disturbing kiss.

"That's a little better. You going home?"

"No. Emily and I are muddling through."

"Turkey dinner?" he asked.

"Ummm-hmmm." She was watching her brushstroke.

"May I come?"

She looked around at him to exclaim, "Why, of course! Aren't you going home?" Surely, she thought, there'd be no harm; Emily would be there.

"My parents are on the other side of the world," he said.

She continued with her painting. "Our Thanksgiving is no big deal anywhere else in the world so they probably just forgot about it."

"They rarely remember me, except to wonder if I've been kicked out of another school."

She looked up. "And have you?"

"No. Actually I'm doing very well here."

"I'm glad to hear that." Her comment was a neutral filler.

"Are you? I'm working, so I can stay around."

She suspected his meaning, but she let it pass. "How do you like this mishmash?" She indicated the huge experiment her group was creating.

As he eyed it, saying her work was better than the others', quiet footsteps in the hall stopped at the studio door and Sara appeared. "Hello," she greeted them. "I expected to find you here." She loosened her coat and pushed off her knitted hat.

"Another orphan?" Piper smiled back at her. "It didn't occur to me to ask if you'd be around. Come to dinner tomorrow?" With Emily and Sara it would be even easier to be with Reg.

"Love to. Thanks."

"I don't believe I know where your home is, Sara," Reg asked.

"Nowhere. Anywhere." Her smile was cynical. "My family is so split and hostile, it's easier not to go anywhere and just avoid the whole hassle."

He nodded in understanding. "I know the feeling."

Dabbing paint and watching her brush, Piper offered, "I think I can promise Emily and I won't quarrel or lecture or scold, but, so you'll feel at home, we'll try to limit ourselves to disapproving sniffs and cold stares. Okay?"

Concealing a smile, he raised eyebrows to Sara. "We can handle that." They exchanged a grin of agreement.

Then Sara stepped back and examined the giant board Piper was working on. "My God!" she breathed.

"Yes," Piper grated. "Fortunately it won't be known as mine. Anyway, Professor B.C. said it was a good experience—several artists working on the same thing—and he said to be sure to notice he didn't say learning experience."

Emily had purchased a second small turkey, and they ate at one the next afternoon. Emily, Reg, and Sara had a great deal in common. Piper listened, very bored. The others discussed music and authors she'd never heard of and didn't care about. Reg and Sara had an impassioned argument over the merits of some piece, and Emily dug up her recording of it; the three sat like stones, listening, exchanging telling glances and occasional nods at vital passages.

Piper cleared the table and did the dishes. Garret called her and said gloomily that he couldn't think of one damned thing to be thankful about, and Piper cried. All in all it was a rotten day for her.

But the other three had a great time. They got into a Scrabble game that was loudly argumentative with shouts of laughter. When they were hungry they moved into the kitchen and ate turkey sandwiches, orange-cranberry sauce, the relishes and pickles and olives, and the rest of the pumpkin pie. When they were finished they continued to argue and laugh while they absentmindedly cleared their plates and stacked them in the empty dishwasher and never noticed that Piper had cleared up after dinner or that she'd laid out supper.

She went upstairs to her studio and drew a picture she called *The Feast*—and it depicted her day. The next day she showed it to Professor B.C., who said she'd captured isolation in the midst of a crowd extremely well, that it would touch a lot of people who'd felt that but had never seen it expressed so poignantly. He looked at her and said she had a great deal of untapped talent, that all she needed was training. "But look at other people too. Paint what's in yourself, but look through their eyes as well."

"I don't see other people's views."

"It will come. You're young. It will come." He showed her some of his paintings. He meant to share them with her, but she didn't understand them. She examined them for a long time, straining. He smiled and said, "You're not alone. There aren't very many people who can share this side of me, but with you, I think that time will come."

He dug around and came up with a very small painting of a tree. "I'd like you to have this. When you're gloomy, look at it."

She looked at it then. It was just a tree. No. It was more. It was alive, growing, reaching up to the sun, spreading out. Rooted, it was still free. "Why, it's"—she looked up at Professor B.C. in amazement—"it's just a *tree,* and you've . . ."

He beamed his best Bill Cosby grin of delight. She'd seen what he'd wanted her to see.

"How can you give it up?" She held it in a cherishing way.

His grin became a serious one. "I've got it here." He touched his chest. "Everybody has problems. Everybody knows what it's like to feel alienated. Everybody needs to adjust his life. It can be done. Anywhere you are, you can grow and spread. You just have to find out how. And there's always someone, somehow, who can teach you or show you the way."

"Emily said something nearly like that."

"It's true." He nodded very seriously.

When she took the painting home, she showed it to Emily, who took it to the wintry window light and studied

141

it for a long time. "That's genius." Her voice was soft. "Where will you hang it?"

"Do you want to share?"

Emily nodded, and they finally hung it at the bottom of the stairs, where they'd see it the last thing at night and the first thing every morning. They stood and looked at it, then they smiled at each other and nodded. She never did show Emily *The Feast.*

The raw cold days arrived. Nothing seemed to stop the winds. Piper complained they came all the way from Alaska, across Canada and the Dakotas, for the sole purpose, in the long trip, to shriek deliberately across the campus at Champaign, Illinois.

Reg scoffed. "You've got to spend a winter in Chicago."

"Why, is it rough?"

"You know they call it the Windy City? They weren't just talking about balmy summer breezes."

There were several days of dusting snow, red cheeks, talk of holiday skiing, and approaching finals. Piper's short story won second place in the writing contest. In addition, the committee made inquiries about her illustration. Would she be willing to submit more work? She replied she was very willing.

Before the Christmas holidays, Reg came to Piper's barren studio and took an old kitchen chair to sit in as he watched her work. After a long time he said, "I'm going to ask Sara to move in with me."

"No!" She whirled on him in anger.

He couldn't hide a small intensely interested smile as he asked, "Why not?"

"Reggie, she's too vulnerable, and you're too uncommitted. You could hurt her terribly."

"She's not a child," he commented.

"But you are." She was really furious. "You leave Sara alone unless you are completely committed to her. I will not have her hurt."

"She seems tough enough to me." Reg shrugged.

"Then you're not looking." She turned back to her easel and went on painting, but her strokes weren't as smooth, and he knew he'd made her furious.

To placate her, he explained roughly, "I told you because I wanted to be sure you weren't available."

She gave him a cold stare. "Do you think it makes it any better that you intended to ask Sara? That she is your admitted second choice? I think it's a perfectly awful thing to do to a woman. And I'm ashamed of you."

For some reason he didn't slam out of the room, but continued to sit there. They didn't speak. She cleaned her brushes, covered her canvas, and began to sort roughly through the papers on her waist-high drawing table.

"When we first met, I was sure I'd get you."

"Then you were deluding yourself," she said through narrowed lips.

Reg turned up his hands in a plaintive gesture. "No one's ever turned me down before. . . . And I knew you couldn't be too indifferent—with that picture you painted of me."

"Of *Garret!*"

"It was my body!" He poked his thumb at his chest.

Her tension and anger mounting, she snapped, "The way I used your body to paint Garret would be like you using a woman and pretending she was someone else. It was cheating, but it was Garret I painted. Don't you forget that." Those last words were like jabs.

"Then why aren't you living with him?" he demanded, challenging her.

She turned from the table, holding a sheaf of papers in one hand and flashed at him. "Because I can't get *enough* of him!" She flung the handful of pages across the small room and glared at Reg as they floated to the floor. "I am consumed with my need for him! My love for him is almost a sickness. I am jealous of his work, his companions, anything that distracts him from me!" Her fists clenched; her eyes flashed; she raged at the startled man. "For our sakes I must be distracted so that he can live a reasonably normal life, and so can I. Otherwise I don't know what shall become of us." And she stood, her chest heaving, her mouth in a tight line, and she added, "Or what will become of me."

His eyes serious, he shook his head. "I had no idea."

"Now you do."

"Your painting was so sensual," he said, gesturing vaguely.

"Only for Garret." She made that clear with a sharp downward sweep of her hand.

He watched the movement of her body. "I wish it'd been me," he said with regret.

"You know nothing about me at all." She turned her back on him. "You'd be crazy to get tangled up with me. Even Garret barely has enough humor and sense to put up with me." She flung out her arms and faced him again.

There was a long silence; Reg put his head to one side as he studied her. "Are you trying to appear unattractive to me?"

She put a hand to her forehead and rubbed it hard. "Actually I'm being unbearably honest. I hate opening myself up this way. No one wants to admit to being a miserable failure."

"Failure?"

"At what they want most. With me it's Garret's time. Period. I would like it if we could be friends, Reg. Anything else is unacceptable."

"Cut and dried?" he queried.

"Yes," she answered firmly.

He smiled slowly. "Hello, friend." He held out his hand.

Before she took it she said, "Don't sleep with Sara. Not until your heart belongs to her."

"Aw, Piper."

"I mean it."

He eyed her. "Poor Garret."

"That's what I've been telling you."

"God!" He shook his head in droll disbelief.

"I'm deadly serious."

"It's been fairly obvious." He put his hands on his thighs and pushed himself up from the chair, but he just stood there.

She eyed him for a time, puzzled, then understanding dawned. "You came for supper?"

"I thought you'd never ask. But, Piper," he complained. "If I have to be lectured every time I eat here, I'm only going to come over every other night."

"Go call Sara and see if she'll come too." Piper bent to pick up the scattered papers.

With elaborate surprise Reg asked, "I have permission to phone her?"

"You can even sweet-talk her. Just stay out of her bed."

"Nag, nag, nag . . ." he said all the way down the stairs.

CHAPTER SEVEN

For the holidays, Reg had a reunion with his parents in California at Lake Tahoe, Sara went to New York, and Emily flew to Mexico with a friend.

Garret came to Urbana. Piper was half-sick with anticipation and clung shamelessly to him at the airport. He loved it and laughed deep in his throat.

Inanely she gasped, "You got to fly again? How did you ever make them let you?"

"I broke out." He put his things into her car, and he drove. It was just as well he did because she couldn't keep her hands off him. She said a good many meaningless "Oh, Garrets" and his eyes glinted and seemed to have flames leaping in them—hot blue flames mixed with gray.

He was shockingly pleased that Emily was away, and he felt he showed great restraint in waiting until they got to her room before he began to make love to her.

When she considered how carefully she'd dressed to go out and meet him at the airport, it was remarkable how quickly he undid her arduously coordinated outfit. She was naked in no time as was he. And they crawled into that big, freshly made-up bed and snuggled down together with sighs and murmurings. Their touching brought exquisite thrills quivering and shivering through their bod-

146

ies. And it was not long before their tempestuous ride soared to completion, at least temporarily.

He leaned over her, letting the cooler air from the room under the covers, so he had to lean on her, and tuck the covers close around their warm snug nest. "I do believe you missed me."

"Ummmm."

"What did you miss?"

"Ummmm."

"I believe you should add speech to next semester's schedule."

"Ummmm." She moved languidly.

"Don't do that!"

She lay still, but she kissed him along his jaw. He moved his budding stubble along her face in gentle circles. "I didn't shave this morning so I could save these up for you." She sighed and moved. He ran his hands over her body, feeling the goose bumps.

"I've missed your whiskers," she whispered sensuously.

"I could have sent you some after I shaved."

"I like them only when they're attached to you." She moved her head to let him reach more of her throat, and she made enticing sounds and her body twitched in marvelous ways.

"So you missed that?" His mouth opened and sucked her earlobe, making her wiggle again. "That too?" And she only sighed in reply.

He took inventory on what she'd missed, having to recheck everything. She said he'd already checked that spot; he couldn't remember. She said he had a short attention span. He asked what about. She giggled, and he blew into her neck and lost track of the list and had to start all over again. He found she'd missed a good many of the things he'd done, then he tried to determine which she'd missed the most, but they both lost track.

The time was idyllic. They decorated a small tree. Emily had left out some lights and ornaments for a much larger one. They used them all and thought the heavily loaded tree just beautiful. They played all the holiday music, had a roast goose and plum pudding, and they wandered through the newly fallen snow. It was a Christmas-card world as snow drifted over the deserted campus like a magic veil. They built a snowman, had cozy fires in their bedroom, and snuggled together in the big bed.

Watching his reaction, Piper showed Garret *The Feast*. He examined it, nodding, understanding. "I know," he said several times. And he was struck by Professor B.C.'s painting of the tree. He felt the same magical communication of life and hope—and anchored freedom.

Once when they were bundled up, walking hand in hand through the snow, and he was being excited over a new, unhappily nameless challenge, she observed, "You really think the world should be geared to men, don't you?"

He shot a quick look at her to see if she was starting an argument, but her face was untroubled. He replied, "I come from a long line of men."

"And surely a few women?"

"There may have been one or two . . ." He looked doubtful, trying to remember any, then he continued. "I belong to the Club of Men. I'm on the side of men running things. I know the arguments and admit some may be valid, but basically I can't see men relinquishing power to women.

"You might make me *pretend* something different, but that's how I feel. You're just lucky I had my crazy old great-aunt Miriam, who was such a nut on women's rights. That makes me put up with your foolishness and not drag you back with me by the hair."

"I can't believe you're saying all this. I suspected it, but I never really thought you would . . ." She was puffing with some indignation.

"I checked you out for a tape recorder when I was helping you put on your jacket. You thought it was simply lust, but it wasn't. It was just a good frisk. This way, when I'm dragged before the Women's Tribunal, if you accuse me, I can always deny having said it."

"Incredible!" she gasped.

"But I must comment that for the radical you are you're in very good control of yourself today. No frothing at the mouth, no fire-shooting sparks, no steam from the nostrils."

After she'd breathed a gust of air out of her mouth so that the cold frosted it and he'd laughed, she explained, "It's because in these last few months I've learned restraint. It's the maturing process caused by association with earnest students."

"Like Reg?"

"And one realizes one must always indulge people whose thought processes are muddled or askew, whose receptive channels are clogged."

"Sounds as if I have a cold." His expression was earnest. "But you must agree that the logical basic organization of civilization is that men rule and women obey."

"You're a true primitive," she declared. "But what about—"

"Anything other than male rule is a fluke attributable to the cracks in our modern society caused by spineless, milquetoast men. It will all be readjusted and things will go back to how they should have been all along."

"Yeah," she agreed cynically. "Like in Iran. It was only two weeks and women were back in the veil, denied schooling, denied choice. My God, Garret, you can't think that's right?"

"Somewhat severe," he agreed. "But . . ."

She went on. "It could happen just that way, and that fast—anywhere! Men still rule us all. Our lives, even our bodies. Just think of the Comstock Law, think of the appalling power the government has over women's bodies. Men again."

"No one can fly in a plane, look down, and not see the staggering extent of civilization without realizing there has to be limits. Birth control is very important."

Her mind ranging, she considered, "No wonder women went into convents. They were probably rebelling against men even then. If we had a daughter, would you feel so in favor of some lug dragging her off to a cave and having total say over her?"

"Wellll . . ." But when she laughed at his hesitation, he reiterated firmly, "Men are the masters."

"I'd probably help her become a nun."

He was amazed. "A Presbyterian nun?"

"It would be rather unique." They grinned at each other. "But you'd think it was all right if your son went out and bashed some little girl over the head and dragged her to his cave."

"Men never hunt women." He stated that positively. "Men are only interested in good government. Women are driven by lust to trap men."

She laughed uproariously. "As with us?" she asked, remembering his relentless pursuit of her.

He became suddenly earnest. "Did I ever thank you for saving me from Barb Tallman?"

"So you knew it was you I wanted to save?"

"Of course," he replied. "You said you wanted to drag me into the bushes and ravish me. For me"—he sighed like a victim—"it was out of the frying pan and into the fire."

"That day on the dock . . . you heard all that?"

"About you wanting to ravish me? Of course." He looked at her. "And the fact it would be worth it to me to have you even though your father would cut me in two with his gatling gun!" He swung his head in a small circle, his eyes wide open, and slowly crossed them.

She laughed at him, and he went on. "Tell me, do you still lie on your stomach groaning, clutching your hands and longing to ravish me?"

"Oh, yes." She heaved a long sigh.

"Then why are we standing out here in the cold?"

Back at the house they had to replenish the wood in the fireplace in the living room, but it wasn't long before he had her on his lap, sitting on the sofa, which they'd moved in front of the fire.

She complained he had cold hands. He chuckled, but she shivered, so he plopped her on the sofa and got the Snug Sack and unzipped it. He settled her back on his lap and they crawled into the sack, he rubbing his hands hard on her flannel-covered back and corduroy-trousered legs.

She wound her arms around his neck, and they kissed. It was very quiet except for the snow-muffled sound of the occasional passing car and the quiet fire consuming the logs. His hands continued their rubbing, but it slowed as the moments passed.

She moved her palms over his cold ears and thought

how interesting that his breath could be so hot while his ears were still that cold.

When he let her up for air as he shifted their bodies she commented, "I feel I'm fraternizing with the enemy."

"No, no," he hastened to reassure her. "Consider you're making the supreme sacrifice—giving your all to sway me to your cause."

Drolly she inquired, "How can I change your mind *this* way?"

Unbuttoning her shirt, he replied ponderously, "True causes take many avenues . . ." His eyes glinted as his laughter rumbled in his chest.

"Think you're pretty funny, don't you?"

"Oh, baby . . ."

She was exasperated. "You always call me baby."

"You're still a child."

"And someone your great age should be able to handle a child and brainwash me into believing men should rule?"

He finished removing her shirt. One arm went around her to pull her close to him, her back was supported by the diagonal band of steel that was his arm, and his other hand slid up over her round, bare breast to fondle it.

"If I'm such a child . . ." She gasped as his mouth explored her breasts, delicately moving his whiskers over that tautened, tender flesh, exciting it.

He raised his head. "Hmmm?"

"What?"

" 'If I'm such a child . . .' " he prompted.

"Oh, yes. Why are you doing these things to me?"

He exhaled a long-suffering sigh. "It's not that I want to," he said in a complaining way. "What red-blooded man wants to sit around in front of a fire on a snowy afternoon wrapped in a woman and a blanket, fondling and kissing and fooling around?"

Curious, she asked, "What would a red-blooded man want to do on a snowy afternoon?"

He replied with patient, practical logic. "Be out in the good air, ice fishing, duck hunting, discussing good government with the other masters, and not be bogged down, sweating it out under a blanket, laboring over domestic affairs." He shifted her to pull her trousers off her hips.

"Oh," she said. "I don't want to keep you . . ."

"No!" He was noble about it. "Duty is duty. One must fulfill one's obligations."

"That's big of you."

And he laughed. "Unbutton my shirt. I would, but my hands are all tangled up with this woman on my lap."

"Yes, master," she answered saucily.

"That's my girl." He rocked them both as he struggled to get his trousers off his hips.

"I could get up." She tried to do that.

"No, no. Sit still. This is excellent exercise for muscle tone." Then he leaned around her, squashing her, while he pulled his pants off his ankles.

"Do you always do it the hard way?"

"Standing up, in a canoe, at night, with a hard wind blowing."

It was some time before she settled down again, and still she giggled.

"One of the nice things about you, baby, is you're so young, all the ancient jokes are new to you." He grinned, pleased.

"That's an ancient joke?"

"It was probably chortled over by the first caveman on an old watersoaked log." He kissed her for a long time,

153

holding her. It was steaming under that blanket. He took both her hands and put them on his hot bare chest, pressing them hard against him, then he slowly moved them down his body. His eyes glinted in the firelight. "I love you, Piper." With her hands on him, he simply sat there, watching her avidly.

Her lips were parted, her hair tousled, her bare shoulders highlighted by the firelight, and she was lovely. He wished he had a picture of her like that, and with that thought he lifted her aside and got his camera.

He had to coax a little, and she blushed, but none of the pictures he took was vulgar, and only one was of her naked, lying on the floor with the firelight touching her body in seductive lights and shadows. He watched them developing and gasped, "Wonderful! Beautiful! Now I'll have a picture of you."

He put them aside and went to her; he leaned down beside her on the rug, looking down at her, his voice husky. "Tell me you love me."

"I love you," she whispered.

He groaned and put his face next to hers, and whispered the muffled words, "Darling . . . dearest . . . my love . . ." He made her blood sing through her body and her bones melt, and her brain go fuzzy. She heard his deep throaty chuckle as he asked, "What's troubling you, baby?"

"You."

"And what do you want?" His eyes held blue-gray fire.

"I'm—I'm trying to think of a way to free you of domestic strife."

His laughter rolled out, and he pulled her to him and began to make serious, passionate, tender love to his wife there on the rug before the fire. And against the window-pane the icy rain began to tap.

The next morning they wakened and, naked, got out of bed to stand by the window, looking out sleepily. The world was covered with ice. Every twig, every wire, every-thing. And still it sleeted. It was a beautiful winter won-derland.

Garret took pictures of that too. "Wait till the guys back in the desert see these. They'll think they're faked. They'll sit there, fanning themselves in the air-conditioned rooms, drinking cold beer, and look at the snow and say they don't believe it. I'll show them these of the snow, but I won't show those of you, since I have no intention selling you."

"Selling me!" She pushed back and braced her hands on his broad muscular chest.

"You being my slave and all. If I am master, and I am, then you are slave." He explained it as if it were complete-ly logical.

"I'll be darned!" She struggled to get away, their bare bodies sliding, touching, and bumping.

He complained, "The training period is always a drag." Then he gathered her close to him and commanded, "Be still! Opposition inflames me; you know that!" He frowned furiously at her. "But there's no way I can make love to you before I have some food. I had no idea, when I came to see you, that college girls just want to lie around and make out. It's shocking." He released her and stepped back.

However, she moved nearer, standing with her naked body almost touching his bare one. She ran her fingers up his back, clasped his neck, ruffled his hair, and kissed his mouth wickedly.

He gasped, "Did I teach you that?"

"Yes, master."

"I'm not sure you have it exactly right. Do it again. I need to check the nuances."

That time she did it slower, suggestively moving her bare body just a bit against his.

His voice was a little hoarse as he commanded, "Again." Then in a while he choked out, "Again!" as he toppled them onto the bed.

She breathed a protest. "I thought you needed food."

He instructed, "In the arduously demanding task of slave-training, one must make sacrifices."

She chuckled and struggled to get out from under him.

In a sharp stage whisper, he cautioned her, "Watch it! Your movements are insidiously sensual."

She erupted in giggles.

He hissed, "That giggling makes you jiggle. Stop it!"

"Yes, master."

"Ahhhh. Kiss me good-bye."

She replied regretfully, "I don't dare!"

"Careful," he warned. "You know what opposition does. When breakfast is ready, call me."

She leaned over and patted his bare tight bottom and pulled the down comforter over him. He smiled, his eyes closed, and by the time she was dressed, he was asleep again.

An hour later she lugged his breakfast up the stairs, wakened him, propped pillows for his back, and placed the tray on his knees. He was delighted, sleepy, and smiling a yawn. She sat and watched his enjoyment of the meal. His hair was rumpled, his eyes lazy, and he would look at her and grin as he ate up every scrap, then sighed in contentment.

The ice storm gave them the gift of an uninterrupted week. They called the Morlings and were sweetly regretful that they were not able to make the trip to see them. They listened to the weather, viewed the magic of the winter, watched old movies on TV, cooked strange dishes, and it was like all the times they'd been together—ideal.

She had his attention. They talked almost constantly now, and they made delicious love. Piper wondered why it couldn't always be that way.

Too soon it was time for him to leave. Salt and sand had been put on the icy roads, and she drove him to the airport for another good-bye. And in no time, she was alone again. Which was better? Seeing him every night for a little while? Or seeing him occasionally for an intense concentrated time?

But Piper, who had left him, knew she could never do without him.

Emily returned tanned and exhilarated from Mexico. The second semester began and Piper progressed in her education. She was a disciplined student, her assignments were organized, and she worked at a steady pace. She was mature enough to appreciate being at school.

Piper's classes in drawing had been like removing a cork from her bottled ability. She reveled in its release. Her imagination ran with her fingers, and she began to turn out marvelous work—work that amused or communicated. She did a watercolor of the desert's subtle shadings, catching the beauty and heat of that harsh land. And there was a figure there, a woman, not lost, but searching for some-

157

thing. That was clear in the pose of her body, the turn of her head, the positioning of her arms.

When Professor B.C. saw it, he smiled and said a satisfied "Ahh." Although several of her professors were standouts, her association with Professor B.C. was especially rewarding. She found he had given away a lot of paintings of trees, and she bought one for Emily.

One bitterly cold afternoon he showed her how color influences how you see a picture. He used watercolors. The time he spent was a gift, he said, when she offered to pay him a tutoring fee. "A gift can't be purchased, it can only be cherished, then passed on to someone else who needs it," he said.

He had a treasured daughter who, Piper learned, had leukemia. She did a quick charcoal sketch of the child giggling and gave it to him. "You caught her!" he exclaimed. "Ah, I've waited with a camera and tried and tried to catch that, and you did!" And he taught her the secret of painting trees.

She sent one of her own to Garret. He called her, very touched, and they talked for quite a while that night. When he said good-bye he mentioned they had a new problem-solver and "Ann" was fitting in well.

"A woman?" Piper exclaimed with a strange still feeling in her stomach.

"Yeah. She's got a mind like a steel trap. I think we ought to have a chromosome check."

"A chromosome check?"

"Uh-huh," Garret explained. "They can take a scraping from the inside of the cheek and tell which it is—male or female. Some years back a communist country was entering very masculine females in female competitions. And they were winning. So they devised a chromosome check to weed out those who'd had sex change operations. As you know, any man can beat any woman."

Somewhat annoyed, she questioned, "So you reject that Ann could be a true woman just because she's bright?"

Complacently he replied, "With a mind like that she must be a sex-changed male."

"You male chauvinist!" Piper exclaimed.

He interrupted, "My picture still there?"

"Yes." But her tone was tart.

"I'd like to crawl out of it and crawl into bed with you."

"Oh, Garret . . ."

"I guess I'll just have to go drool all over your picture. Write to me. I'll call you next week, baby. Think about me."

But that week she didn't think very often about Garret. Her thoughts were buzzing with Ann. How old was she? Was she married? Did she work directly with Garret? What did she look like? What color was her hair? Did she laugh and tease with the men? With Garret? How did she look in a swimsuit?

Her mind built up a prim, spectacled, thin-lipped, bony, humorless woman. But at night she dreamed of a druidess chasing a fleeing Garret, who laughed back invitingly and wasn't running very fast.

Sara climbed the stairs to Piper's studio and sat on the wooden kitchen chair to watch her paint. "Have you heard from the people who wanted you to submit some drawings?"

"They said they'd send me an outline and some ideas of what they want. It's a coffee-table book, whatever that is."

Sara supplied the answer. "Something elegant you display on a coffee table."

"Oh." Then she added, "They said it should be here after the holidays. So, any time now."

"I'll be interested in what you do with it." Sara opened her coat buttons and removed it.

"I'll show you. You're nice to be interested."

"Piper . . ." Having begun, Sara then hesitated.

"Ummm?" She was concentrating on an exact stroke.

"Have you any . . . interest in an affair with Reg?"

Piper glanced up in surprise. "Good heavens, no! Why would you ask that?"

"I just wondered."

Again Piper looked at her curiously. "You can't think I'm even interested in him. Not that way. You've met Garret."

"Yes, but you're here and Garret's somewhere else. You have needs. An affair would be the logical solution."

"For me," Piper declared easily, "it's out of the question."

Sara watched as Piper continued her painting unperturbed. Then she said, "He mentioned before Christmas that I might move in with him. Now he's backing off. I could just go over and begin it, but I've been waiting to see if you wanted him."

Piper put down her brush and pulled her stool over to her. She wiped her hands on a rag and frowned down at it. She perched on the stool on one hip and bent that knee so a heel was on a rung as she studied Sara. "I wish you wouldn't go to bed with Reg."

"Why not? I want him."

"For your own sake. It is the most intimate relationship

160

between a man and a woman, and it should have the most meaning."

"There's the body's needs to consider." Sara was reasonable.

"There's discipline and self-control and responsibility."

Sara grinned faintly. "Fifty percent of all women do it."

Piper frowned at the smile and said sternly, "But then, obviously, fifty percent don't. That one statistic, if it's true, is proof that no matter how you stand on whatever subject, you can quote statistics to back your stand. I said if it's true because I've seen people answer surveys."

"I have had affairs before," Sara admitted, "so what difference does it make?"

"Doesn't it to you?" Piper demanded angrily. "Don't you care about yourself enough to value yourself?"

She shrugged. "I like sex."

"And if you get pregnant, you just simply get rid of it?"

Sara said faintly, "I did get pregnant once."

"What?"

Getting to her feet slowly, Sara walked over to the window and looked outside into the snowy yard. "I really loved him and moved in with him. Then when I got pregnant he said he wasn't ready for marriage. That I'd spoiled our relationship by getting pregnant. And he took off."

Piper shook her head sadly. "He was ready to live with you and have all the privileges of marriage, but wasn't ready to take the responsibility that came with it. What a cheap and selfish man!"

"Yes," Sara agreed, her head bent as she examined her thumb. After a long silence Sara continued, "I was seventeen, on my own, and I couldn't handle a kid. My family is split every which way, so I was completely alone. I lost

161

it before I had to decide between having it and an abortion."

After a pause filled with anguish Piper said softly, "I can't believe you're ready to risk going through that same routine!"

Sara considered the statement soberly, then said, "It could be very similar."

"Don't do it!"

"Well"—she smiled at Piper sadly—"you've given me something to think about. Thanks for listening. I've never told all that to anyone." She moved over to the drafting table before she turned and went on. "Incidentally, the man responsible? I saw him during the holidays."

Piper was silent, waiting.

"He came up to me and said 'Well, hello!' like a long-lost friend. I looked at him, and he was a stranger. I stared at him, trying to see what I'd seen in him. There was *nothing*, Piper, there was nothing at all!" Her voice caught, but when Piper reached a hand out toward her, she moved from it.

She shrugged. "I had lived with him and slept with him and made a baby with him and there was nothing at all. He hung around. There was a party and a lot of people milling around. I knew he would ask, and he did: 'What about the kid?' That's the way he said it. He had the guts to ask. So I raised my eyebrows and replied, 'What? The kid? Oh, that . . . I lost it.'" She laughed bitterly. "He expected to sleep with me that night and couldn't understand why I wouldn't and got mad."

They were silent for a long time. Then Piper suggested, "Let's walk."

They walked through miles of snow before they finally returned to Emily's. She looked at them sharply, then said nothing. One doesn't teach for all those years without acquiring some instinct for troubled students. She simply said, "Supper's ready."

She had a thick stew in the slow cooker, toasted French bread, and put out a blue bowl full of crisp red apples. They shrugged out of their coats and kicked off boots as they somberly sat down at the round kitchen table. Food had been the last thing on their minds. They picked up their forks, ate their plates clean, and sopped up the last bit of gravy with the chunks of crusty bread. They drank the cold milk, ate apples, and their sighs were peaceful. It had started to snow again.

Emily thought how young they were that food could make them tranquil. She fetched her knitting and sat with them in the kitchen near the tiny corner fireplace she'd added some years before. She had built a small fire in it as she'd waited for them to return from that abrupt walk.

Sara watched Emily's busy fingers, the turn of her wrists as she knitted. "I haven't done that for a long time."

Piper almost asked what she used to knit, but Emily was tuned in psychically and just said, "I've the neatest ski cap pattern." She fished through the bag at the side of her little lady's rocker and tossed a folded paper up on the table. Sara bent over it as Emily rummaged further, brought out a skein of raspberry wool, held it up next to Sara's hair, and raised her eyebrows, asking agreement from Piper, who smiled at her aunt and nodded a silent, gulping smile.

Wondering at her niece's emotion, but knowing it centered on Sara, Emily only winked in reply. Then she dipped into the bag again and clattered two knitting needles onto the table before she went back to her own knitting.

After Piper cleared away the dishes they moved into the

living room and settled before the fire. Sara and Emily contentedly knitted, but Piper was restless and moved around. She told the others, "It's really snowing."

To Sara, Emily offered, "We have extra room. Why don't you just stay the night?"

"I'd love it." She smiled and looked so young sitting in the firelight.

"Anyone you need to tell?" Piper asked. "Landlady?"

"Reg," Sara replied.

Emily became alert when Piper swung around, her face distorted with anger. But Sara protested, "No, no. He just comes by and walks me to campus in the morning," she chided, but she was amused.

Head up, Emily tensely watched, then wondered—Piper and Reg? But how easily Piper told Sara to use the phone just inside the kitchen so her conversation could be private. Then when Sara came out, laughing, and said Reg wanted to speak to Piper, alarm again licked through Emily. She strained to hear. But Piper was laughing, then Emily heard Sara speak into the phone as Piper returned to the living room. She grinned at Emily. "He said, 'You don't trust me worth a damn, do you.' He thinks we've taken Sara into protective custody." And she laughed again.

After that Emily didn't need a diagram. This upheaval concerned something in Sara's life. Something probably from the past and no longer a threat or, even at that age, the food wouldn't have soothed them. It was Reg and Sara. Piper was only an interested onlooker, and on Sara's side.

Sara was young and might do well to have someone on her side. Emily went up the stairs thoughtfully, turned on a dim light in one spare room, quickly made up that bed,

164

and turned on the electric blanket so the bed would be welcoming and warm. Then she hunted up a flannel nightgown, laid out towels, and went on to her bed.

After hanging up the phone, Sara returned to the living room. Piper was squatted before the fireplace arranging the logs on their ends so they would stop burning and wouldn't be wasted. Sara stood at the bottom of the stairs, looking around. "It's a home."

"Ummmm." Piper was distracted as she struggled with a clumsy log.

"What makes it that way?" Sara asked.

"I don't know." Piper too looked around.

"I've been in a lot of houses," Sara said. "But very few homes. So . . . what makes it?" She sought the answer to the riddle. "It isn't just the old furniture. It isn't that it's a big, roomy house. It must be who lives in it."

Having always lived in a home, Piper wasn't any help. "Colors have to have something to do with it." She betrayed her increasing preoccupation with her artwork.

"The people." Sara was sure.

Piper nodded. "Emily is special."

". . . and Piper," Sara added.

In the gloomy dark of the next morning they heard the rhythmic clunk and swish of someone shoveling snow. In their separate rooms, the two young women heard Emily open a window and call, "Reg! Stop that this minute! I've two neighbor boys who shovel my walks, and you're ruining our business arrangement!"

Reg couldn't believe that. To make an impression a guy carries things up and down stairs and shovels snow, he said to Emily. How else was he to make a good impression? Did she have anything she wanted carried around?

By that time Piper and Sara were looking down on him too, and he grinned back. In the early light the trees were black tangles of snowburdened limbs and the bushes were black cones that held caps of snow. It was all silhouetted against the snow-white background and the slate-gray clouds.

From her upstairs window Emily intoned regally, "I guess you are here for breakfast."

He drove the shovel into the snow. "I'll start the coffee." He plunged through the rest of the drift to the porch. Having run downstairs barefooted, Sara opened the door and stood back in that long, high-necked, flannel nightgown, her eyes laughing at him.

He'd been stomping the snow off his boots on the porch and glanced up as the door opened to just simply stare at her. Then he stepped quickly in and closed the door. "You'll freeze!" he scolded. "And barefooted! You'll catch cold!"

Saucily she reached over and unzipped his jacket, spread it open and, wiggling, put herself inside it with him. His arms closed around her tenderly, protectively and he whispered, "Oh, Sara."

Later, while the women were upstairs dressing, Emily and Piper stood in Sara's door and Emily said, if she liked, Sara could move in. That could be her room. She should think about it. Then they went to their own rooms and left her there. Sara had been stripping the sheets from the bed. She stopped and looked around the room with a dewy smile—and she remade the bed.

CHAPTER EIGHT

The next time Garret called, Piper grilled him. "What's Ann look like?"

"What's she *look* like?" he asked, astonished. Then he paused and said, "Her hair's that real real light color . . ."

"Blond?"

He considered his reply. "A little lighter."

"Is she pretty?"

He replied, "She's sure got a brain."

"Does she swim?"

"Like a fish!" But he was becoming impatient. "I didn't call you to talk about Ann."

"No. Well." Then she babbled, "Sara moved in here last week. You know how quiet she's been. Well, she's so funny and I think Reg is courting her seriously."

He grated, "I didn't call to talk about Sara and Reg either."

"Oh, Garret . . ."

"For Pete's sake, don't start that Oh, Garret stuff."

She gulped and couldn't think of anything to say.

"Baby," he said very tenderly.

"Oh, Garret . . ."

"I love you."

"I love you too." Her voice was watery with tears.

"I hope you're doing as well in your classes as your letters and drawings to me. They're just great. I can't begin to tell you how much it means to me to get your letters, but they're no substitute. We can't go on this way," he warned.

"Garret . . ."

"I've got to go. Be sure to have the oil changed in your car."

"Oh, Garret . . ."

"I love you, baby. Good-bye."

That same day she lost a carefully typed article she'd written that was due. She searched and searched and was cold and miserable and found it in the slush. She took it to her professor and he listened to her and watched her woebegone face. He wondered if she had enough starch for journalism. But he told her to retype it and have it in the next day.

She sat up all night typing and sniffling, turned it in the next morning, went home, and crawled, shivering, into bed. She just missed catching pneumonia. But Sara got it, and then Emily.

They all dragged around feeling rotten. Reg came over, hearty and cheerful, and fixed their suppers. Between classes he did their shopping and ran errands. He offered sponge baths too but couldn't convince any of them. He supplied them with flowers, an armful of jonquils that must have cost a small fortune that time of the year, and a pot of vigorous chives that graced the kitchen table. Then each one got a small bouquet of rosebuds and baby's breath, and he found a pot of parsley, then an azalea. He was very sweet to all of them, but he was particularly cherishing to Sara.

* * *

With the four of them as a basic group, they went in fluctuating numbers to just about everything offered by the different schools at the University. They went to all the games, shows, and exhibits and to the musicals and musicales.

The others relished the musicales, but Piper fidgeted through them until she took pad and pencil and drew the musicians. Then she took her drawings, exaggerated them, and did a pen and ink of an entire group that Professor B.C. loved. He hung it in the next month's student show, and it outraged, offended, or delighted most of the music department; and Piper had enough requests for copies that she made a deal with the print shop. And she sent a copy to Garret.

He wrote that they were busy and he missed her badly, only he'd mis-typed it "bedly," or had he?

Piper received a set of galleys of a fantasy from the publisher who had seen her illustration for her prize-winning short story. They wanted to see what she could do with illustrations for this story. Since the drawing was in the way of being a submission on her part, they would not pay for her time, nor would they guarantee that she would get the assignment, therefore they suggested she do one or two drawings and send those. Then she should wait until they contacted her before she did any more.

She avidly read the story, handing the pages to Emily, who skimmed them before giving them to Sara.

"Do the cover," Sara suggested. "Make it smashing."

"Can you do a shipwreck?" Emily asked. "That would be smashing."

"I can fake anything," Piper said confidently.

169

"What about the subject for the cover?" Sara wanted to know.

Piper replied instantly, "When he first sees her."

"Perfect." Sara clasped her hands together.

Emily argued that nothing could be more smashing than a shipwreck, but they ignored her.

Carrying the galleys up to her studio, Piper cleared the drawing table and took a piece of butcher paper to begin sketching her ideas for the cover—all small doodlings about two inches square. She turned her head, considering, crossed some out, then went on. She ended up with three she liked. She cut those from the sheet and pinned them in a row on the corkboard that she'd nailed to the wall above her drawing table. She looked at them for a while. Then she smiled.

Garret wrote they'd missed the Saturday night buffets so much, that he'd started having them again. He was chief cook and bottle washer and the food could never compare to hers, but Ann helped.

That letter sent Piper out for a long, angry, jealous walk to work off her temper and indignation. When she returned to her studio, she drew Garret chased by the druidess—him fleeing in terror, and she a ragged, ravening nightmare, with a gaping, toothless mouth and warts.

The drawing was about two feet high and one and a half feet wide. She watercolored it with painstaking malice, and pinned it onto her corkboard. And even that gave her pleasure.

However, Sara eyed it later and commented that she thought any of the three little sketches for the book was superior to that one.

Sara too paid Emily what it would have cost her to stay

at the dorm. She really didn't think it was enough, but it was hard making Emily consent even to that. Reg offered to move in too and, however unsuccessfully, he argued so eloquently that Emily thought he should think seriously about law after he finished his M.B.A.

"I'm going for a master's in business?" he asked, surprised.

"Of course." Emily went on with what she was doing, so obviously there was no need to discuss it.

"Well if that's the case," Reggie said, "then I think I'm going to have to study harder."

"Naturally," Emily agreed.

Then he wanted to study there. Emily said no, he could come for supper, but study dates were a mistake; you neglected either the books or the girl, and neither benefited. She had noticed his grades could be improved, therefore he must not be distracted when he did study, therefore it was logical he should study alone.

"Noticed my grades? How did you notice my grades?"

She gave him a quelling glance. "I looked them up."

That made him so indignant and uncomfortable that he made Sara laugh.

Garret wrote that he too had been ill, and about the same time Piper was. It must have been a psychic phenomenon. Some strange bug had really laid him low. He'd had nightmares and once he'd knocked Ann clear across the room. Ann had been a brick, nursing him, risking getting it too, but she hadn't. Along with being a brain, Ann was as healthy as a horse.

Piper cried. Garret had never been sick the whole time she'd known him, and now that he had been, another woman was there to nurse him. Sara and Emily argued

171

with her that that didn't mean anything. If Garret was talking about Ann nursing him, Piper should realize there was nothing underhanded. And Piper wailed.

That night in bed Piper stared at the picture of Garret looking at her, and she wondered if Ann had ever seen him that way . . . and she soaked her pillow with her tears.

Piper's submission drawing for the cover picture of the fantasy was completed and sent. It was gorgeous. The awareness between the man and woman was vibrant, and the lines were beautifully done. She'd had the print shop reproduce it for her, gave a copy to Sara to thank her for her interest, and she'd sent a copy to Garret.

One night after supper Reg told Emily and Piper that he was going to marry Sara. They weren't terribly surprised.

"Where would you live?" Emily inquired.

"You mean we can't live here?" Reg was indignant. "The only reason I'm marrying her is to move into this house! I've been trying to live here all along, and you wouldn't let me. So I figured if I married one of you, that would be it! I know I'd have a hell of a time convincing you, Emily. All you want to do is argue and regulate me. Piper's married, so that left Sara. And here I make the supreme sacrifice . . ."

And Sara put her head back on the chair and just laughed. Reg and Piper were carried along into her hilarity. But Emily never flicked an eyelid. She just went on knitting and observed, "There are the maids' rooms in the attic, but there's no kitchen. Just two rooms and an antiquated bath. But there're the cook's quarters over the garage. There's a living room and bedroom on either side and kitchen and bath in the middle. That could be cleaned up and made usable. But you'd have to promise to mow the yard and shovel the snow."

Reg pretended to be disgruntled. "I thought you had that farmed out to the neighbor boys."

"I pay cash," Emily instructed. "I'd give you living quarters in exchange."

"You do know money's no problem?" He questioned Emily seriously.

"Lawn and snow are." She examined the piece she was working on. "You could endow a scholarship on what you save in housing."

"Done." They beamed at each other. Then he shifted and rubbed his hands together, having closed the bargain and asked, "How soon . . ."

"Have you asked her?" Piper inquired.

"Oh," he said dismissively. "That's no problem. She's putty in my hands, and I can convince her in ten minutes. We'll get it all arranged and then we'll just let her know where to be when."

Piper frowned. "Sara, do you know he sounds remarkably like Garret?"

Lazily she asked, "Does he?"

"Sara . . ." Piper began, but Sara had her chin on her hand and was watching Reggie, very amused.

Later Piper asked Sara, "Are you sure?"

"Oh, yes." She smiled at Piper very serenely.

"Does he know . . . about . . ."

"He knows it all. That's why he was so glad when I moved in here. He understands. His life has been a taste of mine."

They survived February. Like any Northerner who survives February they all felt they had accomplished something. It was so bitter and icy and cold and mean, but they made it through. The days passed and Piper continued to expand as an artist. Her mind pictured what she wanted, and her hand drew it, and she never lost the wonder that it was so.

With the second semester half over, Piper learned how interesting journalism was, but it was not for her. It was drawing and painting that filled her. And when she'd lose herself in it to the point that Emily or Sara would knock on her studio door and demand she come to a meal, and she was startled the time was gone so quickly, then she began to understand Garret.

Having received the commission for the drawings for the fantasy, Piper finished them in a surge of delight. Then the publisher sent her two other books to illustrate, and invited her to submit a painting for a cover of yet another. Coupled with classroom commitments, the amount of work scared her at first, but she was disciplined, eager, and so engrossed in her tasks that she only occasionally surfaced into the real world. Then she truly realized what Garret's work was to him.

As Sara and Reg worked to get the garage apartment in order, Sara told Emily Reg had only half-kidded all along when he'd campaigned to live there. That caused Emily to shake her head in wonder that she could attract such devotion. Later she told Piper that it was she who made that house a home. It had always been empty and cold until Piper moved in. Piper questioned, surprised: "Me?"

And Emily elaborated. "Your mother's training. You're truly your remarkable mother's daughter. Did you know I introduced them?"

"Mother and Dad?" Her mother was so different from Emily. How could they have been friends?

Emily explained. "Soon as I met her, I knew she was just the one for your father. He was a rake and a rogue and I knew . . ."

"Dad?" Piper questioned Emily in great unbelieving surprise, sure she hadn't heard correctly.

"Oh, yes. A complete playboy. We thought he'd never get straightened out."

"*Dad?*"

"Yes! Your father! My brother!" Emily almost shouted in impatience.

Piper was astounded. "I can't believe it! He's so strict!"

"He began to change the day you were born, and he's kept getting worse. A complete metamorphosis. It was a miracle."

"I can't believe it!"

"Well, believe it! For God's sake, Piper, I've told you about twenty times! At any rate, I introduced them, and he fell head over heels in love. They knew each other six weeks before they were married."

Piper gasped. "Six weeks?" And she sat down with a thump.

"Yes." Emily frowned at her. "Hadn't you ever known that?"

"They never mentioned it." She shook her head as if it'd come loose.

Doggedly Emily went on. "After the first week, all your mother did was cry, and your father stormed around demanding they be allowed to marry. Her parents were obstinately opposed. They knew his reputation, you see . . ."

"Six weeks!" She was still hung up on that part.

"Yes," agreed Emily, then she added with telling drollery, "Twice as long as you and Garret. I suspect they had reason not to tell you, and I forbid your mentioning it to either of your sisters, do you understand me, Piper? This is serious."

"I promise—six weeks!"

Since the next year Arlene would be coming on campus, and also living with Emily, she and sixteen-year-old Jennifer visited during spring break from high school. Arlene floated around the campus eyeing the clothes on the coeds and assessing the quality of the male student population, and Emily said thank God Piper would be there next year to wield some control over her sister.

Jennifer clinically evaluated Sara and Reg and decided they were well suited and the marriage would be a good one. They replied well, thank God for that, and now they'd go ahead with their plans. Jennifer nodded sagely.

With serious, squinting eyes, Jennifer thoughtfully reviewed Piper's pictures hanging around the house and studio. She called the one of Garret great. "Other than a penchant for addle-headed females," she pronounced, "and being too old, he is almost ideal."

Piper told Jennifer that she had no business snooping around her room. That made Arlene smile wickedly and ask how Piper could sleep with that picture right there at the foot of her bed looking at her that way. Then Piper scolded Arlene about being bold and smart-mouthed, all of which caused Emily to roll her eyes a little more.

Then Jennifer soberly studied Piper's other paintings. She allowed she could see signs of maturing. That was all to the good, and she requested a painting of a tree. Although Jennifer judged Piper wasn't yet as good as Professor B.C., she was coming along. That information was relayed by Piper to Professor B.C., who chortled and asked if there was any possibility of his getting Jennifer into an art class.

Piper replied that at the moment Jennifer was going for political science and then law. He nodded, his eyes danced, and he said, "Generally that kind goes for social work."

During that time Garret phoned. "I feel like I'm on the other side of the moon," he began despondently.

Suspicious, Piper demanded in shock, "Are you?"

"Not quite."

It wouldn't have surprised her if he had been. She thought the government capable of it. "Are you all right?"

"Just about."

"Just . . . about? Are you sick?" Her voice rose in alarm. She didn't want him sick with Ann taking care of him again.

"No, I'm okay. It's been so long since I held you, I've forgotten what you feel like."

Her knees buckled and she had to sit down. "Oh, Garret . . ."

He groaned. "Me too, baby."

They talked about nothing that was important to them. She told him Reg and Sara were progressing on cleaning up the apartment. She had some illustrations to do. She didn't tell him her parents had only known each other for six weeks before they married, nor did she mention her father's early reputation. It was bad enough he knew that her mother squealed when her father rubbed her with his whiskers. They were just too scandalous to be parents.

177

He said he'd been jogging and swimming and playing a lot of bridge because Ann loved it.

"Bridge?" Piper couldn't assimilate that; he loathed bridge.

"Yeah. There's not a whole lot to do around here."

After a pregnant pause she said her sisters were there to visit the campus. "Jennifer said Reg and Sara suit each other and will have a good marriage; so they said okay, they'll go ahead with it."

Garret laughed; he thought that was funny. "God, but I miss you, baby."

But when they hung up, Piper sat there looking at the phone and wondering if Garret was real.

She took Arlene and Jennifer back home and stayed for the weekend. Surreptitiously Piper examined her parents and weighed their exchanged glances and decided Emily had exaggerated. Her mother wasn't the weepy type at all, and her father raging with passion? Nonsense.

Piper's painting of Garret was exhibited in the Year's Best Student Show. It was gratifying that the comments she had were of the skill, balance, perspective, and brushwork. There had to be a few whistles, but those were from the women. That made Piper wonder if women clamored after Garret all the time. And he was playing bridge to please Ann. Would he have played bridge to please her? He hadn't even shown up for dinner to please her! What did Ann have?

And worse: Were they having an affair? Garret was a very passionate man. Ann had nursed him through that illness, and he played bridge to please her. That was no casual friendship. Jealousy crawled through her veins and curled in her stomach, and she was sick with it.

178

With finals coming up, she worked very hard, lost some weight, and was distracted and preoccupied. Emily and Sara exchanged glances over her in a concerned way, but she wasn't aware of it.

Sara had entered a competition in her journalism class, and won the right to go to Washington, D.C., to do an interview. She had to pay her own way, and she asked Piper to go with her. It would be a break and, anyway, Piper had never been to Washington. They said it would do her good to go.

Their plane landed on that postage stamp in the Potomac called Washington National Airport. They were met by an Illini Alumnus named Meg Tower. She was an aide and general gofer connected with the Senate, who helped to smooth the paths of visitors from home.

She'd set up an interview with the senior senator from Illinois, and he was very gracious to them. They sat in on a news briefing at the White House, and they received invitations to attend a banquet for the editors of small-town newspapers.

When Sara and Piper met Meg at the hotel where the banquet was being held, they found the woman in a dignified boggle. They figured she'd seen some remarkable happening, for she'd appeared unflappable up until then.

Meg explained she'd been in the White House at the end of a private ceremonial that involved a study team of some sort. "There were several of them, and the woman must be especially bright, for the President gave her an award. But the whole point is, one man accompanying her was *fantastic!* And not only that, but I just saw that group being cosseted outrageously as only visiting royalty is, and they are in one of the smaller rooms down the hall from the banquet! If we leave the banquet early—right after we've eaten—we can hang around in the hall so I can drool."

"I heard there was a shortage of men out here," Sara said to Piper.

But Meg babbled on. "Wait till you see this guy. He's married, and he carries his wife's picture around. That may seem ordinary, but *his* picture is an oil painting!"

"How romantic," Sara laughed.

Meg half-closed her eyes in an attempt to look mean and crafty and said, "I hope she's dead and he's ready to quit mourning."

That made Piper exclaim, "Why, shame on you, Meg!"

She shrugged. "It's that or go to hell for coveting."

"Wishing her dead has to be as bad as coveting. Who is he?" Piper argued.

Meg admitted, "I don't know. The whole thing's been very mysterious. I tried to find out, and they just said 'Security.' His hair is almost white, bleached out by the sun because it's dark underneath."

Entertained by her, Sara asked, "How old?"

Meg admitted, "He could be any age—it doesn't matter."

"My, you are selective!" Piper teased her.

"Just wait. You'll see." Meg was positive.

They asked to be seated just inside the door, and periodically Meg popped out to check on the progress of the people down the hall. The others at their table thought she wasn't feeling well. When she came back and hissed, "Now!" the others at the table gave her such sympathetic looks that Sara and Piper had a great deal of difficulty acting casual about their departure.

"They aren't quite through with dessert." Meg was a little breathless, while Sara and Piper were smothering giggles as they tried to tell Meg about the discreet table conversation on travelers' woes which they were sure had been triggered by her abrupt departures from their table. But Meg wasn't giving them any of her attention.

While Sara regaled Piper with a replay of the diners' words and nods, Meg stood against the wall, tense and alert. Then she hissed, "Look! There he comes!"

And Piper turned with a smile that fell as she gasped, then she yelled, "Garret!" and lunged for him.

Startled, he hesitated only a second, then rushed the necessary steps to meet Piper halfway. He gathered her to him and she clung there as he kissed her endlessly.

One corner of Piper's dazed mind heard Meg say, "Damn, she's alive" in a very disgruntled way. And she heard Sara laugh.

Someone pried them apart and talked to them. It was an old, gray-haired lady who was very amused. Apparently by then she'd already met Sara and Meg, for they were talking and visiting together like old chums. Meg wasn't very animated, but Sara was having a good time. The old woman said good-bye to Garret and kissed him. She then patted Piper's cheek and wished her well. "But with Garret you don't need any luck. He's a marvelous man. We shall miss him." Then she and two men went on off down the hallway, turning to wave before they went out of sight.

"Who was that?"

"Ann."

"Ann?" She looked back down the hall, incredulous. "That old lady?" And again she heard the bubble of laughter from Sara, who leaned to kiss her cheek, and they went off too, leaving Piper standing alone in the hall with Garret.

He said, "The President gave her a decoration. She solved a problem we've had for over a year."

"She did?" Piper was befuddled.

Garret said, "She sure as hell did. I couldn't believe it. I told her. What are you doing here, baby?"

"You call her baby!" Piper exclaimed indignantly.

He demanded, "What are *you* doing in D.C.? I've a plane out of here in the morning. What if I'd missed you? I would have had Emily up on top of the drapes! My God, woman."

So she began to explain between kisses just what she was doing there until some man in pajamas opened his door and suggested with forbearing patience that they go to the lobby for their chat.

Garret agreed, but as they walked toward the lobby he said, "I have a room at another hotel; let's go there."

She whispered, "Mine's in this one. I've got the key right here." She opened her bag, dropped it onto the carpet, and everything spilled. They bumped heads getting down to scoop up the contents.

"What about Sara?" he asked.

"She has another room."

"How wise," Garret intoned.

"Yes, sir."

"Meekness drives me crazy," he reminded her.

She smiled slyly and breathed, "Yes, master."

In the lobby, waiting for the elevator, they stood in the crowd with some decorum. "That old lady really was Ann?" Piper wanted to know. "The one you played bridge with?"

"Uh-huh."

"I thought she was blond." She watched her husband's face. "Why didn't you say gray?"

"I said it was lighter than blond." They walked into the elevator, rode in silence, and finally reached her room.

Sometime after they'd closed the door, Piper gasped. "I can't breathe."

"Later," he replied. "Oh, baby . . ." He said that four or five separate times while he touched her. He groaned that he seemed to remember her being that shape, but he hadn't been sure he hadn't dreamed it.

She murmured she had to get out of her heels because her legs weren't working right, and she felt very wobbly. He said wobbly women excited him. She mentioned again that she couldn't breathe, but he was breathing fast enough for both of them. As passion swept through her, she began to make strange little sounds and her hands moved in odd, fluttery ways, and her breathing became gaspy.

"Are you all right?" he whispered, a little concerned.

She gulped a strangled "Yes."

"What's the matter?" His voice was a little rough and hoarse.

"I guess"—she whispered and swallowed noisily—"it's just that I want you so badly, I'm getting desperate."

His voice was a low soft purr in her ear. "Oh, you do? Well, well. But then, what can I expect of a girl whose mother squeals when her husband rubs his whiskers on her throat?"

Almost panting, she admitted, "It's worse than that!"

"Worse?" he encouraged.

"They knew each other only six weeks," she blabbed. "And my mother cried five of those and Dad stormed around demanding she be allowed to marry him, and before that he was a rake."

"No!" He seemed unbelieving. "Whatever will our children be like? We're just lucky I have such solid conventional genes."

She nodded in agreement, then added, "But there was that idiot great-uncle of yours." After that he kissed her, and they lost track of everything but sensation, and their thinking became disconnected.

Just to be together . . . to be close again, to have their hands on each other, holding each other, their mouths tasting each other's lips again. It was as if time went askew and nothing else mattered but their loving. Their passion, their need for each other raged, burning for the release of their uncontrollable love.

She exclaimed "Oh, Garret . . ." in many ways as he worked his magic skill on her, unknowing of her own spells that wound around him, entrapping and enchanting him. The touch of her hands made him gasp and groan as she shivered with desire. And they were immersed in the sensual flood of passion that flowed over them to drown them in timeless love.

It wasn't until sometime in the middle of the night that they got around to reasonably coherent conversation. They talked so easily now, as easily as she'd always wanted, sharing their time apart . . . sharing. Piper realized then that in the last year, each time they'd been together, the sharing part of their visits had expanded. The ten-year gap in their ages had narrowed as their closeness grew and in the years to come, they would grow closer. Garret had even come to understand her need to be useful, that as a person and a woman she had that right.

Finally Piper asked how long could he be with her. Then she didn't wait for his reply, but went on. "I can't let you go, Garret . . ."

"I'm not going anywhere . . ." he began assuring her.

But she wasn't listening, she was so intent on what she was saying. "I love you so much, I can't divorce you or leave you or let you leave me or whatever it is we've been doing. I'll go anywhere with you, and I'll figure out a way to survive. Emily and Professor B.C. said there are all sorts of ways to extend an education. I have to go back for finals, but then I'll go wherever you are and live with you and be your love . . . and I promise I'll be contented if you'll just come home at night."

"Well," he huffed. "That's just great! And what am I supposed to do with my mornings and evenings?"

"Huh?"

"I've quit my job."

"You *haven't!*" She was aghast.

"Yeah." He frowned at her lack of enthusiasm. "Are you that fond of living in the desert?" That seemed impossible.

"Well, but, Garret, your work means too much to you. I can't let you give it up just for me." She now realized she could go back and live in the desert to be with him, for now she could cope with even that.

"I'd do anything to have you with me again. I love you, Piper," Garret said firmly.

Their kiss was marvelous and they repeated it several emotional times with the murmurs of love and devotion that are generally an unvoiced assumption between couples.

When she figured out what they'd been talking about, she took it up again and asked, "Are you really serious? Have you quit? You don't have to, you know, I can survive anywhere now as long as you're there."

That touched him to his heart, and they shared more

exquisite kisses. Then he told her the job was with an electronics firm. "In Dallas."

"Texas?"

"There's a Dallas somewhere else?" He pretended to think about it.

"And you'll come home now and then?"

"Why?" he asked, his voice turning into a silken purr. "Is there something at home I'll want to do?"

"Well . . ." She traced a finger through the wiry hair on his chest and made little circles. "There might be."

"Oh? Really? What?"

And she showed him.

Almost nine months later to the day Garret called the Morling house near Springfield, Illinois, and spoke to Mr. Morling. "Hi, Grandpa. I especially wanted to talk to you. We have a perfect, beautiful little daughter; and I'm calling to ask you about a gatling gun."

LOOK FOR NEXT MONTH'S
CANDLELIGHT ECSTASY ROMANCES ®

A woman's place—the parlor, not the concert stage! But radiant Diana Ballantyne, pianist extraordinaire, had one year before she would bow to her father's wishes, return to England and marry. She had given her word, yet the moment she met the brilliant Maestro, Baron Lukas von Korda, her fate was sealed. He touched her soul with music, kissed her lips with fire, filled her with unnameable desire. One minute warm and passionate, the next aloof, he mystified her, tantalized her. She longed for artistic triumph, ached for surrender, her passions ignited by Vienna dreams.

$3.50

Vienna Dreams

by JANETTE RADCLIFFE

Candlelight Ecstasy Romances

THE DARK HORSEMAN

Marianne Harvey

author of *The Proud Hunter*

Beautiful Donna Penroze had sworn to her dying father that she would save her sole legacy, the crumbling tin mines and the ancient, desolate estate *Trencobban*. But the mines were failing, and Donna had no one to turn to. No one except the mysterious Nicholas Trevarvas—rich, arrogant, commanding. Donna would do anything but surrender her pride, anything but admit her irresistible longing for *The Dark Horseman*.

A Dell Book $3.50

"THE MOST ROMANTIC NOVEL SINCE LOVE STORY"
—Good Housekeeping

Change of Heart

SALLY MANDEL

Once in a long while, a story is so bursting with tenderness that its charm is irresistible.

That story is Sharlie and Brian's story. Change of Heart— a love story for a lifetime.

$2.95